ISBN:

ACKNOWLEDGMENTS

No book is published without the help of a team or experts; and I have been very fortunate to have an extraordinary team of skilled friends and professionals help produce Tam's Journey.

To Debbie Woods for her photography and friendship.

To Carol England, Sandy Golnick, and Linda Nowell, for your enthusiasm, ideas and encouragement.

To Ruth Campbell, Carol Herndon, and Paul Bennett, for your careful proof reading.

To Tommy Raiguel, for his layout and attention to detail.

And finally, to Linda Lysakowski, for her editing, expertise, and belief in my writing.

You all have lifted me up and helped bring Tam's story from the fairy world to the human world. May your lives be filled with fairy magic.

DEDICATION

To Mr. Walter Blair

I never learned anything in Mr. Blair's fifth grade class, nothing I could hold in my hand, nothing I could keep in my mind, but something I'll hold in my heart forever, and that is love.

From all your students over 35 years, thank you, Mr. Blair.

With love,

Jill Raiguel

BOOK 2 IN THE FAIRY FUNDAMENTAL SERIES:

TAM'S HUMAN: ANOTHER TALE FOR ALL BEINGS

By Jill Raiguel, MS, MFT

Illustrations by Sean Segarra

PROLOGUE

A stiff breeze blew through the Grand Meadow and indeed through the whole Fairy Kingdom. The giant everlastings stood proud as if waiting for something special. Even the sipping birds rustled their blue/black feathers and looked Tam's way as she approached.

Tam flew slowly to the Grand Meadow's Center and yelled, in a very un-fairy like manner, "I'll take the assignment, Great Fairy."

Hearing those tinkling bells, Tam looked around. The Great Fairy drew near her and she floated up to Tam.

The Great Fairy said softly, "No need to yell, I'm right here."

"Greetings, Great Fairy. I'm a bit nervous," Tam said.

The Great Fairy answered, "That's very human. Humans are often nervous when they are starting something new. Are you ready?"

"I am!"

The Great Fairy pulled out her wand from what looked like her sleeve and began to tap Tam on the top of her head. "Become human size, become human size."

Fairies always and forever repeat things twice. And Tam began to spin slowly at first and then faster and faster. She saw swirls of neon colors: reds, pinks, greens, and blues.

"Tam, you will have all your fairy gifts and fairy help. You will have all your fairy gifts and help. The Creator will be watching over you."

While Tam's body stretched and grew larger, Tam asked, "Are there any other fairies who have lived as humans?"

"Yes!" the Great Fairy said. "There are some who have chosen to continue to live as humans."

"Why?" Tam asked quickly.

"Does that surprise you?" Tam didn't know quite what to say.

The Great Fairy said," Tam, everything you need is inside you; everything you need is inside you. You are loved beyond measure, you are loved beyond measure."

With a final tap of her wand, the Great Fairy kissed Tam on the forehead. In a half nothing, Tam was gone.

Tam pressed her nose to the Metro's window as the city sites sped by: freight trains, junkyards, skyscrapers, freeways, and cars without number. They whizzed through her mind, too much to take in all at once.

What am I doing here? What am I doing here? What am I doing here? thought Tam.

But the train's click-clack, click-clack rocked and soothed her. The city sites gave way to the suburbs: fences, gardens, small houses, and backyards. Glass buildings, brown haze, and gray cement faded into green grass, blue skies, and pick stucco. She marveled that some yards even had swimming pools. The dappled afternoon sunlight played on her face until she couldn't keep her eyes open anymore. Occasionally the deep train whistle blew and startled her wake.

What is my assignment? What is my assignment? What is my assignment? thought Tam.

Soon the train's hypnotic click clack, click clack lulled Tam back to sleep. As the train pulled into the next station, it passed the abandoned citrus packing houses, the new apartment construction, and stopped cars waiting for the Metro to pass. She couldn't tell how long she been napping when the conductor nudged her arm gently, "Clear Mountain, Miss, this is your stop."

Before Tam was fully awake she and her bags were standing on a platform alone. She turned to face the hundred-year-old train station, new pink stucco and tile roof. Despite the recent remodeling, the clock was still stuck at 12 noon. The train whistle blew and startled dozens of pigeons nesting in the roof, and Tam stared at two stone carved statues framed the doorway to the street. Tam took a deep breath and walked through the stations' archway.

"A rose garden. How lovely!" Tam said.

Tam moved closer to the little park just north of the station. Junipers trimmed set the edges, a few crepe myrtle trees -- red, pink, and lavender -- dotted the sidewalks beyond the grass. The town had built a band shell on the south end for summer concerts, but in the middle low box hedges formed a small walking maze.

Setting down her bags, Tam was drawn to the hard dirt path; and she wound her way to the center in a few minutes. To help her shake off the train's insistent rocking, she would have flown through her home forest, done a few barrel rolls, and finished with several loop-the-loops. But she had to settle for this simple walking meditation. Oddly, it centered her just as flying did, and it connected her to the ground. When she did arrive at the maze's center, she found three rosebushes -- one pink, one red, and one white -- planted around a granite plaque. It simply read: TO MY BELOVED BEATRICE WHO LOVED THE ROSES.

"He must have loved her very much," Tam said out loud.

Feeling more like herself, she walked briskly out of the labyrinth and fingered some fuzzy purple blooms; she scanned the blue rosemary; she breathed in the colors of the pink, peach, and lavender primulas.

"I smell orange blossoms," Tam inhaled deeply and looked around. She focused on the mock orange bushes hugging the crepe myrtle trees, then she let all their scent and colors vibrate through her. And finally she surveyed the town neatly laid out beyond, her new home. "This town must love flowers and plants; it will be a good place to be of service."

Tam's Lesson

CHAPTER 1: THE NEW TEACHER

"I'll bet this new substitute won't last the day." Marv Burton slapped a $10 bill on Mrs. Wagner's desk.

"Put your money away. Let's give this poor young woman a chance; I have a good feeling about her." Mrs. Wagner, the school secretary, replied as she put another ream of white paper in the copy machine.

The heavy metal door swung open; Tam walked in and set down two tan suitcases. She stretched her arms just as she used to stretch out her wings in the Fairy Kingdom. She was not used to carrying things never mind anything heavy.

Pushing up the sleeves on her pale green jacket, the school secretary said, "Welcome to Clear Mountain Middle School. I'm Mrs. Wagner. Now that you have the job, just sign your name here, and we will have a contract. Tell me how you spell your last name again?"

Last name? I do not have a last name, Tam screamed in her mind. A sick feeling raced from the pit of Tam's stomach to her throat. She wanted to run out of the office and get outside to the treetops. She took a long, slow breath just as Grandmother Fairy suggested. Then, another voice within her urged: Calm *down. You are among friends.*

Swallowing hard, Tam grabbed the edge of the desk. Then she managed to say in a normal tone, "Could you repeat the question?"

"Why, yes. What is your last name, your family name?"

"I see.... last...well..." Tam's eyes roamed around the open office. She scanned this new territory just like she scanned the forest for a hummingbird or a squirrel. Then, Tam eyed a very tan worker fixing some electrical wiring. He flashed a supportive grin that looked exactly like The Fairy Coach Rupford's. Seeing that famous, however rare, Rupford-like grin gave Tam a burst of confidence.

Without another thought Tam said, "Rupford! My last name will be Rupford." Tam dropped her hand on the desk making a gentle plop. That was final.

"Sounds like you're saying it for the first time," sensed Mrs. Wagner.

"Well, in a way..." If this woman only knew how right she was. "In a way, Mrs. Wagner, this is the start of a whole new life for me. I intend to make the most of it; to do my best work."   Tam did not feel quite so alone.

"I can see why Dr. Krause hired you. Being a substitute is a roller coaster ride. That class has had five subs, they are a little rough," Mrs. Wagner declared. Tam gulped and tried to stop her hands from shaking. "You'll start subbing for Mrs. Brockway tomorrow morning. But first, the hard part...all these forms. Don't worry, I hate forms too. Just sit right here, and I'll guide you through the whole thing." As the friendly school secretary placed each form on the desktop, Mrs. Wagner's kindness eased Tam's fear. "Just sign here." She said.

Tam smoothed out her navy pants, pulled down the matching top, took a breath, and took the first paper from the woman's hand. She tried not to panic. Instead she fixed on the crystal around Mrs. Wagner's neck. Tam could feel the comforting vibration as she focused on it. She thought of cool blue lobelia, of fluffy clouds on an especially blue day, anything blue to calm herself down.

"You like my crystal? My daughter gave it to me," Mrs. Wagner said smiling.

"Oh, yes, I feel its power to focus thoughts," Tam said.

"Really? Most people do not have any idea the friends that crystals can be," Mrs. Wagner replied fingering her necklace. "I always feel better when I wear it."

"Of course you would, you..." Tam's voice trailed off. Mrs. Wagner opened a folder and sorted through a stack of more forms.

Tam thought: *This human uses power of positive thought and focalize with crystals. I wonder if she uses color to revitalize as we do, if she knows to take the crystal off when she is ill, if she knows how to clear it. I had better not discuss any fairy practices just now; not before I have even started my new job.*

The three freesia blooms on Mrs. Wagner's desk caught Tam's attention, as she drank in their perfume and let their rich yellow vibrate through her. The yellow reminded her of her Fairy Coach Trella's golden wing color.

"My other daughter gave me the freesia. I love the smell, don't you?" Mrs. Wagner fingered the leaves lovingly. She inhaled their fragrance. Then, she sneezed. Mrs. Wagner took a tissue from the box and blew her nose. "Allergies, you know."

"Where I come from we do not have any allerg..." Tam thought better of saying that as well. Instead she closed her eyes and said softly, "Where I come from we have flowers in bloom all the time. It is good to be around flowers and the scent of nature."

Mrs. Wagner replied, "Well, you must have a nice garden back home. You'll probably like our ecology club.... Now, dear," Mrs. Wagner looked over the top of her half glasses as kindly as Grandmother Fairy, "Tam is short for Tamara, right?" She typed it in the blank. "Do people call you Tammy or Tamara?"

I guess I just make this up as I go along. This sweet lady will tell me if I am out of order or break a rule. Tammy.... Tamara.... I like the way Tamara rolls around in the mouth.

Tam straightened up as she did in the Fairy Kingdom when she wanted her full height and shouted, "I like Tamara!" The other two women sitting at their desks looked up.

"No need to yell; I'm right here." Mrs. Wagner patted Tam's hand as if she were comforting a distressed fairy flapping her wings. "Tamara, I'll just fill out most of this for you. Why don't you stop by my desk tomorrow so you can look it all over?"

A slender man in tan slacks and a brown T-shirt walked up to the desk. Mrs. Wagner pointed her ballpoint toward the man and said, "Marv Burton, this is our next substitute teacher, Tamara Rupford. Tamara will be taking Mrs. Brockway's place; she's having another boy, you know. Marv Burton is your department chairman. He'll show you around and give you your keys."

Marv Burton extended his right hand, as humans tend to do, and stated brightly: "Welcome to Claremont High School. How about a little tour?" Tam held out her hand and allowed Marv Burton to shake it. Then, Mr. Burton held the door open for Tam; and they both stepped outside.

CHAPTER 2: CLEAR MOUNTAIN

To breathe fresh air again. The blue sky and horse tail clouds, one of my favorite skies. Those mountains look close enough to touch.

Indeed the San Gabriels did look close and clear this January day. The winter rains had turned their dark blue slightly green; snow dusted the peaks. Some days the smog dropped a fine haze over them. When the smog was especially thick, one did not even see these rugged mountains. But today Southern California was at her best washed clean by the Santa Ana winds. Suddenly, she heard a calamity of voices talking all at once:

"I am her Fairy on Assignment…No, I am!... You never finished the job properly the first time."

As Tam turned to look over her left shoulder, Mr. Burton asked, "Are you looking for something?"

"No! I just, I thought I heard something." Tam tried to cover up her distraction.

Again Tam glanced over her shoulder and then at Burton. He clearly heard nothing, but Tam heard familiar voices arguing heatedly:

"I'm the most senior fairy here. I should sit on her left shoulder. I'll give the coaching. No, I'll do..."

After several moments, Tam blurted out, "I do not want you around when you behave like that."

The fairies fell silent. Mr. Burton stared at Tam puzzled and said, "I hope you are not referring to me."

"Oh, no." Tam was horrified that she had offended her new boss. "It's these new clothes. I feel like my skin is crawling with bugs."

Half-kidding and half-serious, Mr. Burton said, "You are not hearing voices, are you?"

Tam hesitated...Then, in a flash of Tam brilliance, she stated matter-of-factly, "Why, yes! I do hear voices. I have that... what you call it...Extra Sensor...." She laughed out loud.

"ESP. Oh, yes, I see." Mr. Burton laughed to see that Tam was just kidding. He could not know that she did indeed hear many, very real voices. "I'll just be a minute," he said.

While Mr. Burton stopped to talk to another staff member, Tam took the opportunity to say under her breath softly, but sternly:

"Fairies, get yourselves organized. I still do not know what in the Creator's name I am doing. I need a human coach who can tell me how humans do things.... Like how to walk in these awful shoes." Tam's ankle turned over in her new shoes just as Burton said:

"Miss Rupford, this is Coach Harwick. Tom is our baseball coach, and he tries to teach P.E." He slapped Tom on the back gently; they had taught together for many years. Deeply tanned, Tom stood in white shorts and white T-shirt. Tam had taken off her shoe and held it her right hand. Now, she tilted to one side.

The coach held out his hand, "Tom Harwick. Don't bother to shake hands. New shoes?" Pointing to his, he added, "Now, here's what to wear on your feet, tennis shoes. Happy feet make a happy teacher."

Tam managed to say, "Thank you. Now that is very friendly and very helpful." Somehow Tom's ease and ready solution melted away the awkward moment. "I am Tam...Tamara Rupford," Tam stammered. She dropped her shoe and extended her hand to Tom's.

"Try not to forget your name," Tom said lightly.

"I was just thinking I need a coach."

Mr. Burton smirked, "Miss Rupford is taking over that class that's gone through four subs."

Not fully understanding, Tam had both shoes off and wriggled her toes in the grass.

Tom said, "SHOES AT ALL TIMES."

And unseen voice said, "Be yourself."

"BE YOURSELF? Come on now. I am supposed to teach. Find out what I teach and who? Get out of here! Oh, and get me some of those shoes," she ordered pointing to Tom's feet. "Now, his coaching was useful."

Tam did not see Coach Harwick placing ten dollars in Marv Burton's hand betting on how long this sub would last. Instead she sought a moment of rest under a pine tree. She sat down and spoke quietly:

"Dear Evergreen, I do not see any everlastings or tree giants, but your needles tell me you must be related. Let us be friends." Barefooted, she rested her back against its trunk and closed her eyes. Inwardly she thought: *Let me slow my breathing down and listen to the trees if only for a moment. If you have any wisdom to give, I need it desperately.*

The fairy voices continued talking among themselves:

"Tam is right. We do not know how to coach a being who can talk back, who can see us, who indeed is one of us."

"Indeed, we have no experience supporting a fairy in human form."

"But we still know how to help her in fairy ways. She is tired; I know what will revive her." Tam heard their gentle chuckling that sounded more like rustling leaves than voices. Her eyes still closed, she stretched out for a quick sunbath.

Only the fairies could see the pink cloud that enveloped Tam. Then these invisible magicians added golden sparkles. The strain left Tam's face, and a peaceful smile graced her lips as she drank in the energy.

After several minutes, a fairy's voice said: "That should perk her up. Pink for love and reassurance and golden sparkles for energy and confidence. Better than those powder drinks that so many humans are gulping down."

Another fairy voice added, "Let us not judge human ways. They do not know how to focalize the Creator's energy that is all around them, so they think they need those weird drinks. They just do not know any better."

The other fairy stated, "Tam is correct. Our standard fairy magic is not enough here."

"Exactly my point. We had better get some coaching. I know of only one other being who has served as a human. You stay here and I will be back shortly."

"Right." Only fairies could see the iridescent color of vibrating wings, could hear the faint humming. One of them imagined the Fairy Kingdom, closed his wings to transport, and slipped through time.

Just then, Tom Harwick sauntered over and gently pulled on Tam's big toe. "Hey, you take sun baths on the job? Usually I take them at the beach or in my backyard. Dr. Krause won't take kindly to her staff sunning on campus."

Tam sat upright and answered, "It is another rule? I just needed a few moments."

Coach Harwick squatted down next to Tam and said, "If I can catch a 10-minute nap mid-day, I can go another 12 hours.   Just don't sleep in the middle of the quad."

"Yes, I see. SHOES AT ALL TIMES and NO SUN BATHERS IN THE QUAD. Two Teaching Fundamentals."

"You could say that," declared Tom. "You certainly do have a different way of looking at things. Have you ever substituted before?"

"Never!" If he only knew. "Are the rules all recorded somewhere.... so I could learn them all at once. Where I come from...in my family, we have a book of rules, fundamentals. We learn them from the time we are little," Tam said referring to Fairy Fundamentals, of course.

The bell rang, Tam jumped and stood up. A swarm of students poured out of the classrooms. Girls and boys, chattering among themselves, walked quickly with backpacks, T-shirts, and jeans or shorts. A pair of friends was so involved in their conversation that they almost knocked Tam over with their books. Tam tried to figure out where they were all going. Five minutes later another bell rang, and the campus was quiet again.

"Well, this will be an easy ten dollars," said Tom Harwick. "Some rules are written in the school handbook, but others...others you just have to pick up." He got up to leave and added, "I'll see you.... I'll check on you after your first day. The first day can be murder on subs. If you survive that, you'll live." He laughed as he turned and marched across the blacktop toward the gym.

Tam said out loud: "Oh, fine. I am going to get murdered the first day."

A fairy responded: "Humans are fond of saying one thing and meaning the opposite. It means it will be hard, but you are up to it."

Now a single fairy's wings hummed with delight at being of service.

CHAPTER 3: THE QUAD

Tam brushed the grass off her pants. As she slipped her shoes back on, Marv Burton came walking toward her. During their stroll across the campus Tam noticed several cement block structures built around squares. Within each square was a grassy area or a garden. Classrooms all faced these squares.

Marv Burton explained: "We have five classroom buildings called quads. You will be teaching in the 800 quad. Our horticulture class has just finished relandscaping it. Doesn't it look great?"

"Gardening! I love flower gardens." Tam was delighted that humans were planting and appreciating nature. And, so close to her room.

The horticulture class had made a new curved path through the quad with three wooden benches. Fresh wood chips covered the bare ground. Their scent reminded Tam of her forest home. Three fishtail palms, taller than the roof, guarded the entrance to the quad. Their giant fronds looked like they had been cut in half; that gave them their fishtail appearance. The gardeners had planted several three-foot high king palms in the center. Their blue green trunks looked like bamboo, and their graceful fronds curved around and made a ball that almost touched the ground. Around the base of the palms the gardeners had planted Mexican purple sage, orange and yellow day lilies, and a low bush with a fuzzy plume that Tam did not recognize. Purple blue ajuga spikes covered the ground. The student gardeners had added more color with hanging baskets of red and pink ivy geraniums.

Strange as all these plants were, Tam felt comforted. She needed to be near nature since, for her, being indoors felt so confining.

"I am delighted to have things growing just outside my door." Then Tam saw a strangely familiar tree. "What is that tree? It looks like a cross between our rope and helter-skelter trees."

The trees over in the south corner grew old knotted trunks that twisted and turned like fairy rope trees and had hanging bark like helter-skelter trees.

"Those are very old tea trees," Marv answered staring at her. Her innocence and enthusiasm for such little things puzzled him. She seemed a bit odd, but he found her refreshing. Marv Burton stopped at one door and pulled out an enormous key ring: "The more important the person, the more keys you have," he quipped.

"I see," Tam stared at the mass of metal in his hand. "You must be very important."

"Yes, it is a good idea to agree with your department chairman."

"Another Teaching Fundamental, Marv Burton?" asked Tam innocently.

"Absolutely! Call me Marv." As Marv searched for the right key, a young woman carrying a pile of papers started to open the room next door. Marv said, "This is Tamara Rupford. Tamara is the next sub for Mrs. Brockway." He rolled his eyes.

"Hi," said the woman peering over her papers. "Victoria Moreno.... Glad to meet you." Tam gasped and put her hand over her mouth. "Is there something wrong? You look like you've seen a ghost," Victoria said.

Tam could hardly believe her eyes. Rarely at a loss for words, she could not think of anything to say. She stammered, "Oh, it… it's just that....."

"I know. I look like someone you know. People tell me that all the time."

"But you do… You are my former..." Tam caught herself. She could not say that. Her mind raced. *Is this some kind of joke? … No ...No... Everything has a purpose. I just need to figure this one out. This must be a part of the Creator's plan.*

"Whatever I can do to help you get settled, just let me know," smiled Victoria. Her words brought Tam back.

"Vicki has been teaching for ten years. She's a veteran; she knows all the tricks of the trade. Just don't set her class on fire."

"Right! The last substitute had a student who set a trash can on fire." Victoria finally managed to unlock her door. Tam rushed to hold it for her.

"Say," said Mr. Burton. "I saw your bags in the office. Do you need a place to stay?"

"Yes, I do! I just got off the train," said Tam.

Tam waited a few minutes in the hall gazing up at the mountains. She noticed their tops were covered with strange white stuff Tam had never seen before. Soon Victoria came out.

"Marv tells me you need a room. I have an extra one. It isn't much, but it has its own bathroom and its walking distance to school. I'd be glad for you to stay with us."

"I'll take it," declared Tam.

"Don't you want to see it first? We live right across from old man Matthews but he won't bother you. He hasn't spoken to anyone since his wife died; the poor man hasn't been the same since," said Victoria.

"I know it is perfect!" Tam exclaimed.

"This one's got spunk!" said Mr. Burton folding both hands across his chest.

CHAPTER 4: FAIRY GARDENING

In the meantime, a stiff breeze stirred the Fairy Kingdom's everlastings. If one listened to their soft roar, one could hear a sound not unlike waves crashing, then it faded away. Another giant puff blew through the everlastings sending its roar through the forest again.

Pink peonies stood like cabbage roses, their fragrance sent the bees dancing. Today, yellow plumes of scotch broom and smiling blue and purple monkey flowers carpeted the nearby Grand Meadow. At the far end, in the wetlands, grew stands of reeds and cattails. The sipping birds were bobbing there, as they always did in the early morning, their long white curved bills drinking in the still water, then bobbing up, then sipping again. Wading near lily pads that covered one corner of the pond, they carefully picked up their webbed feet as they searched for breakfast. An unseen presence disturbed them; they flapped their dark blue wings showing their opalescent feathers.

Growing straight up from those pads bloomed red and deep lavender flowers standing on sturdy stocks. A fat frog perched on one pad, waiting to catch his breakfast.

Near the edge of the wetlands stood the rope trees where Grandmother Fairy and The Fairy Coach Rupford played when they were young. The rope trees' rough trunks twisted horizontally along the ground and then up at odd angles. They looked like the Creator had braided great ropes together, so young fairies could and did find them perfect for climbing. Their sword-like leaves hung in bunches.

This morning Grandmother Fairy and the Coach met at their favorite tree limb, as they did every morning since Tam had been on her new assignment, to greet the day before morning tea. Now arm in arm they watched the Creator splash the sky with divine oranges and pinks and reds that blended together. As the sun was ready to break over the horizon, golds lighted the bellies of the clouds. Just as the sun broke over the pond, the dawn's light raced across the water. It was a new day.

Then, they journeyed the short way to the Fairy Coach's cottage for chamomile tea. On the way to the Coach's front porch, they glided by those funny looking helter-skelter trees, their branches pushing out in all directions. These crazy creations had bark that hung loosely like old rags.

Yesterday morning the Fairy Coach was planting blossoming pear trees in front of his cottage. Their delicate white flowers fluttered in the breeze. As his fairy gardeners watered each tree, he called the spirit of that plant. He held out his right palm, and a tiny tornado of light appeared in his hand.

"Give long life to this pear tree," he smiled. The light tornado jumped into the tree. He repeated this process so each tree had its own spirit. He then floated over to the delphiniums; bright purple, midnight purple, light blue, royal blue, and even white ones stood on either side of the porch steps. Again, he held out his hand and a tiny blue tornado danced in his palm.

"Go!" And the light jumped into each towering blue stock. Honeysuckle vines crept around the delphinium spikes; their sweet tang filled the air. The clematis wound up the cottage posts and almost covered the roof in her pink and white blossoms. Blooming in two shades, the pink and white clematis was still demonstrating that Fairy Fundamental: ALL BEINGS HAVE LIMITLESS POSSIBILITIES. The spirit of these plants energized them so they produced huge blooms much larger than any in the human realm.

Now along the path to the Grand Meadow Center marched snowball hydrangeas always in bloom. The fairy gardeners just finished planting brilliant blue lobelia trimmed each hydrangeas bush. This season the Fairy Coach and his helpers added giant gladiola -- pinks, reds, purples, and magentas. Their spikes pierced through the clouds of white hydrangeas. The white background made the glads' colors especially vibrant.

The Fairy Coach hovered over each plant lovingly, and its spirit appeared in his hand. On the Coach's command, it twirled into its flower. When he called the spirit of the hydrangeas, white light emerged. Each gladiolus had a vibrant red or purple or magenta spirit that eagerly swooped into its very own plant.

"Bloom with long life and joy," said the Fairy Coach. His garden, as well as all the Fairy Gardens, brought endless joy to the Fairy Kingdom that spilled over into other realms. When his labors were done, he glided to his porch to survey his gardens. The Fairy Gardeners joined him.

"This season I name you: THE GARDEN OF ENDLESS VARIETY."

CHAPTER 5: FLOWER LESSONS

After his greeting was done, the Fairy Coach pushed his hat back and wiped his brow with a bandana. He then flew to another part of the garden to continue training several future Fairies on Assignment. He waved his hat for them to circle around, and a dozen fairies from every corner of the garden dashed to school.

His double wings buzzed so fast that most fairies could not see their clear green, the teaching color, with silver, the truth color, edging his wing tips. As he glided over to one flowerbed, seven or so fairies fluttered behind him to catch up.

"Now gather round, Green, Orange, Red, and all of you," he barked in his familiar raspy voice. Most young fairies were downright afraid of him; they even called him crotchety behind his back. He picked his way carefully through the greenery and stroked a sword-shaped leaf.

"These leaves belong to day lily. Day lily has exquisite blossoms. Let us see if she has one for us to enjoy today." The Coach looked stern as he eyed the flowers; the fairies joined in his hunt for a bloom.

"I see one," declared Red, as he jumped up.

When Red successfully passes his second level, the Great Fairy will tune him to a finer vibration: vermilion, or garnet, or scarlet, or magenta. His wing fibers will tell the Great Fairy just what vibration will help Red fulfill his destiny. Until the Rose Pool Ceremony, Red and all these fairies still answer to their primary color names; Red, Blue, Yellow, Green, Orange, and Purple.

"Yes, here it is," announced the Fairy Coach as he flashed a quick grin. "Now, see this extraordinary work of nature. She has three waxy petals, each as big as a fairy's fist; this one is gold yellow. He continued, "Day lilies live one day only, just like some people. The rest of their lives are planning for that event; or spent remembering it."

One Fairy raised her hand. After the Fairy Coach nodded acknowledging her, she said, "Like a human wedding or the birth of a human child. Is that what you mean, Fairy Coach?"

"Yes, very much like that. Some humans plan and save their entire lives for one day in the sun, like day lily, here. Then when that wedding, or birth, or graduation has come and gone, they wither and fade; like this bloom, nothing left to live for."

"Life has so many moments to enjoy and appreciate," said another fairy.

The Fairy Coach smiled knowingly, and walked over to another flower.

"Then, we have the mombretia, long elegant leaves much like gladiolus. When she is in full bloom, there will be twelve or fourteen tiny flowers on this stem, that last for several months…and what else?" encouraged the Fairy Coach.

A green fairy answered, "She lives her life over a longer time; she has many exquisite gifts to give, not just one."

The Fairy Coach stood with his hands clasped looking around his lush garden, "I think we have guests."

With that special sound that only fairies can hear, one opened his wing pod. He stretched out and reported:

"Good day, Fairy Coach," stated Pink. Fairies always and forever greet each other.

"Good day to you," said the Coach. "Join our little botanical talk. We are discussing day lily and mombretia."

Pink said, "That is one of my favorite lessons."

"Perhaps you can tell us which flower lives her life more fully?" the Coach asked.

Surveyed the fairies present, Pink suggested, "I'll bet these intelligent beings know the answer." Several enthusiastic fairies raised their hands letting their wings hum urgently.

"Sir, the mombretia because she lives her life to the fullest," answered Yellow. The Coach paused and paced back and forth as he liked to do for dramatic effect.

Pink interjected, "I disagree," as he winked at the Coach. He paused letting his point sink in just as the Coach did. "You see, although daylily only lives one day, for her, that moment is splendid." The young fairies looked confused.

The Coach asked, "Then, how do we apply this to human lives?"

Red continued, "I believe I know, sir. Some humans live like day lily ...for one day in the sun. They waste all those other days waiting or remembering."

"Exactly so, Red," said the Coach pleased but trying not to show it. "Humans average 70 to 80 years, very short lives compared to fairies. They do have the luxury of years and years, and thus many riches and challenges and gifts and losses. Red, the problem is worse than living for only one day. Some humans merely watch others live."

"How sad!" said Green.

"Tragic, really! Now, many of you will be assigned to human charges that are in this condition. How can we fairies help?" This stumped them all. After several minutes the Coach said, "I can see you could use some time to think this through."

The Coach put his hand on Pink's shoulder. Truth be told, he was very proud of Pink for asking to be reassigned to Tam, but The Coach would never say that.

"Before you begin your report, there is someone who would like to join us." The Fairy Coach closed his eyes and said firmly, "Nelson, I have need of you." The power of his words alone brought his top aide.

In a half nothing, the Administrative Fairy Nelson appeared. He did not transport, using his wing pod as other fairies did; he was just there. This skill meant he ranked higher than a single winged fairy, but not yet a double winged. Nelson stretched his iridescent wings, then bowed.

"Good day, Nelson. Please tell Grandmother Fairy to meet us at the Grand Meadow Center. We will hear report today in the traditional manner."

Nelson bowed again and was gone. His elegance, his formality, his swiftness amazed the young fairies. In awe, they stared at the space where he had just stood and vanished. "When I return, fairies, we will continue."

CHAPTER 6: PINK'S REPORT

The Coach flew easily to the Meadow's Center. Pink followed. As quickly as he imagined it, the Coach's silver and green striped canopy appeared supported by four wooden poles. Then, two carved chairs, one slightly higher than the other. Really, these chairs were stools so winged beings could sit on them.

Just as the Fairy Coach seated himself, a luminescent wing pod appeared. Pink, the Coach, and ever-serious Nelson looked toward the familiar hum. Because she was a triple, she had to open her wings slowly one pair at a time. Her first were the color of dawn; next, the color of sunset; then finally the purple ones, a shade from another world. She vibrated them so fast the fairies could not see them at first; then she slowed them down and flapped gracefully. Their remarkable iridescence caught the morning light as only fairy wings do.

She paused and looked lovingly at each fairy, then she said, "Good day, Pink, and of course, Nelson. Good day, Rupford."

They all answered, "Good day, Grandmother Fairy."

"A great day, isn't it?" she breathed in the air taking in the Grand Meadow.

"Leuria, great day to you," said the Coach Rupford. "Please be seated so we can begin."

"How can you know if it is a great day if you do not look around and enjoy it?" She smiled knowing she was making him uncomfortable in front of the other fairies, but they had been such close friends for eons. He let her and her alone get away with teasing. Because he chose to ignore her.

"Let us begin this morning's report," he declared. As he spoke he took off his straw hat and held it up high. It seemed to be taken by an invisible hand. Then, with a flick of his wrist, a green visor appeared with the letters FC stitched in silver. He pulled it smartly over his forehead. Nelson hovered at the side ever ready if needed.

Pink told them what they had observed and how they had helped Tam so far. Then he added, "We have a problem, she talks back."

The Coach took off his visor and roared with laughter.

"That is our Tam, is it not?" smiled Grandmother Fairy. "How did you find her?" Grandmother wanted to know since she loved her great-great granddaughter the most of her 1330 grandchildren. And, she had had no word of Tam since she had left on this most unusual assignment.

Pink continued, "She is well. She has a little trouble adjusting to her human size and weight. She is always pulling and adjusting her clothes. Truth be told, I think she would like to rip them off and go flying up into the trees. "

"Yes, of course; you would too," sympathized Grandmother.

"She has made friends with the teachers and found a place to live," added Pink. "We gave her a pink color bath with gold sparkles for confidence."

"Good," said the Coach. "Where is Rose?"

"I left her watching over Tam," said Pink.

"Good procedure," replied The Coach.

Pink continued, "Sir, how can we help Tam when she can see us and talk back to us?"

The Fairy Coach stood up declaring, "Stand your ground, do not be intimidated. Like a lot of beings, when she is scared she acts angry. Speak the truth."

Grandmother Fairy added, "Remember, Tam needs you. As tough as she may appear, she is scared."

"There are many human teachers all around her who will help with that. You can remind her about Fairy Fundamentals," the Coach stated. "The students have limitless possibilities; their hardships are illusions; in truth, life is easy."

"You mean Fairy Fundamentals apply to humans as well as to us?" Pink asked.

"Yes! Yes!" said the Coach flatly. " Tam must let the children know that she loves them. The human children may not believe her at first; they can be quite thick-headed."

"It is the same as any assignment then?" asked Pink. "Except we have Tam." Pink seemed strained.

"Indeed you do," comforted Grandmother Fairy. "In time, as humans evolve, we will have more of them who see us as well as hear us."

"So I guess we had better get used to it," said Pink a bit frustrated.

Grandmother stated, "When she needs help, you can ask on her behalf. The Creator listens especially hard to those who ask for another."

CHAPTER 7: FAIRY INSTRUCTION

As The Coach and Grandmother Fairy floated to the West Garden, they let the sun's nourishing rays warm their wings. She did not have to say that she was worried about Tam; he did not have to say that he would watch over Tam as if she were his own. Indeed he would go to the human realm if he had to. As they eased toward the pansy beds, their wings beat as one.

"Great day, young fairies," announced the Coach. "Grandmother Fairy is joining us for our lesson." Leuria surveyed the young fairies.

"Great day, Grandmother, Coach," said the fairies all together. They were all sitting cross-legged in front of the pansies. These pansies grew twice as big as ones in the human world. Each color carefully arranged in its own bed. The Creator painted the golden yellow ones, with brown faces; the purple velvet ones with black faces; the sky blue ones, with dark blue faces; the pale orange ones with a color unknown in the human world. Red was leading this morning's lesson in calling in the spirit.

Standing over the purple velvet pansy, he held out his palm and closed his eyes. In a half nothing, a tiny purple tornado of light appeared in his hand, he smiled triumphantly.

"Go home to your flower," said Red. The light jumped into its home flower. The fairies' excitement sent ripples through their wings. "Now you try it. Ask the Creator for the spirit of that flower and hold out your right hand."

All the fairies obeyed squeezing their eyes tightly as if that would help. After a few moments…. nothing. Then all tried again. Only the young yellow fairy opened her eyes to find a lovely blue light tornado in her hand.

She beamed, "Go home," and the light energy jumped into the sky blue pansy nearby.

Red said, "Relax. Yellow let the Creator's light flow through her. You are trying too hard. You must get out of the way, and let the Creator work. That is what we mean when we say: Let the Creator work through us."

Grandmother Fairy drifted to a spot close by, stopped a foot or so off the ground and observed. A flutter went through the young wings.

"Very good job, Yellow," Grandmother said proudly. "Soon you will all be able to call the spirit. It will be as natural as flying. And I have a feeling one day we will be able to call the spirit for humans too."

"You mean some humans have no spirit?" asked Red. "How awful!"

"Some have lost their spirit, too many I'm afraid." Grandmother Fairy looked sad.

"Yes! Yes! Let us continue with yesterday's lesson. Leuria, do speak up if you have anything to add," said the Coach Rupford giving her a wink. He causally reached down and touched a pansy's yellow face; it seemed to perk up as he did. And indeed they all did.

Then Orange jumped up to get a closer look at Grandmother's triple wings. He burst out: "Grandmother Fairy, I have never touched…" and he could not resist touching Grandmother's wing tips.

The other fairies gasped as the Coach barked, "Sit back down at once."

"Rup, it is alright," Grandmother soothed. "How will the young thing learn?" She lovingly took the fairy by the shoulders. "Now, Orange, you must always ask to touch a fairy's wings. It shows respect."

"Orange was dazzled that Grandmother Fairy was so close. But Grandmother's warmth and kindness made it easy to ask: "May I touch your wings?"

"Yes, you may." The young fairy poked at Grandmother's giant wing tip and pulled her finger back quickly. "It is alright. They are very sturdy. Rub them between your fingers and examine both sides. See those veins? Those are my very own wing pattern. You have one too like no other." The other fairies strained to stay seated but were dying to join Orange. "Well, come on, all of you." That sent the group scampering up to Grandmother and surrounding her.

The Coach took off his visor and threw it down in disgust. "You indulge them so."

"They are only youngsters. How can they learn except by asking questions and making mistakes? They need to see and touch and feel life, Rup, not just
observe it. Is not that this morning's lesson?"

"Yes, yes," and he picked up his visor, brushed it off and it disappeared. From the same invisible place just above his left hand, he pulled his straw garden hat out of thin air. The young fairies were so transfixed on Grandmother's swaying wings that they did not notice his bit of fairy magic.

"May we touch them, Grandmother?" asked shy Yellow standing right on a pansy. Most of these young ones had never been so close to a triple-winged fairy. She let her six wings breathe like elegant butterflies.

"But you may want to step to one side; you are squashing poor pansy." Yellow's wings began to flap in distress.

Grandmother Fairy took her by the shoulders and looked into her eyes deeply. "The pansy will be fine, but you are most upset. Learn from your mistakes and go on. Do not let them stop you." She patted Yellow on the head tenderly. "Now, Yellow, may I touch your wings?" Yellow nodded.

Gently, Grandmother took both her hands ran them along Yellow's outer wing ribs. She examined the veins closely, and looked into the sturdy yet gossamer membrane.

"Yellow, I have looked into the fiber of your wings; I see a fairy of great strength and courage." Yellow stared at the ground embarrassed. "I speak plainly because the Coach tells me you all are about to take your second level." The other fairies nodded. Grandmother continued, "So you must start acting more like your true nature. Let your feelings go quickly. You cannot be of service to others if you are overcome by failures and feelings." The young Yellow trembled with fear and delight; she stood her ground and did not let her wings flap.

"Yes, Grandmother," mumbled the other fairies.

Staring straight at Yellow she stated, "Be courageous!" The young, meek fairy pushed out her chest and beamed a much more confident smile.

"Yes, yes," said the Fairy Coach some frustration sneaking into his voice. "I have been trying to teach that lesson for weeks."

Grandmother Fairy wrapped her wings around Yellow and giving her a hug. "Perhaps that is why the Creator sent me here this morning. Sometimes whispering speaks louder than yelling." She winked at Coach Rupford who knew she was talking to him. Yellow looked as if she had grown several inches taller. And, if height were measured by self-confidence, she had. "Now, Coach, you may continue with your lesson."   The Fairy Coach continued, "As I recall we were discussing what causes certain humans to suffer so...Oh," he put his hand to his cheek mockingly. "I have given away part of the answer.... I mean what keeps certain humans from participating in their lives?"

Yellow, feeling much surer of herself, answered, "Fairy Coach, on my observations, I have seen humans sit in front of little boxes with lighted screens for hours."

The Coach sat back on his fairy haunches, and reflected, "Yes, yes! You are on the right track. They even play games on them."

Red piped up, "It is so. I observed two young brothers playing some kind of game, laughing and fighting and laughing again; all the while just staring at the lighted box. The box's high-pitched squealing was horrible."

"Those young bodies are not running outside and soaking up the sunlight," added Orange.

"Yes! Yes! Correct!" He stood up and flew around the seated fairies and hovered next to Yellow.   She was not distressed; she felt somehow the Coach was noticing her.... And, he was. "Now, what can we do to get them into their own lives?" asked the Coach.

Yellow began again, "We have to get them outside, exercising, flying around... that is if they had wings." She let her wings flap imitating flying.

"But that box saps their energy and dulls their minds. They forget who they are; and they do not feel connected to all that is, to their Creator," The Coach explained.

Orange merely said again, "How sad! Then a pink wash or a blue bath or a yellow rinse will not do!"

The Coach answered, "That is true; sympathizing and comforting is not enough in this case."

"No, I am afraid not. We need more than color healing here," said the Coach.

Grandmother Fairy joined in now, "What if I told you the Coach wanted you to replant his entire west garden by dawn?" Her right arm swept across the whole area.

Orange said, "We would have to act quickly, to work very hard."

A light of recognition went on for Red: "Yes, I see! The humans, these humans, need a problem to solve. Such a project would pull them into activity and away from the light boxes."

"Yes! Yes!" declared the Fairy Coach. He tried pouting like a human. "The best solution is action."

"The trick is to create something that is urgent to them. How about some examples?"

Red chimed in, "A human needs to mow the lawn before it starts to rain," added Yellow now standing close to the Coach.

"Good! Now, how about a more serious example?"

Yellow took a step forward and stated, "My charge needs to visit her sick friend." She paused and thought a minute. "And she is the only one who is bringing him food."

Grandmother added, "Excellent! You see how human problems are really blessings in disguise. They get humans into their lives; they can become of service to others." The Coach grinned quickly but all the fairies saw him. They smiled back. But then the Coach said with all seriousness, "Think of ten such problems, big or small. I think that is a good place to end our lesson for today.... Class dismissed."

A riot of wings took off heading for the forest.

After the young ones flew back to the forest, Leuria whispered, "Red and Yellow will be called to the Rose Pool soon." Rupford nodded. He took her arm, and they flew slowly over the garden toward the rope trees.

CHAPTER 8: GABRIEL

Tam, carrying her tan suitcases, and Victoria, carrying her always-huge pile of papers, walked the four long blocks to Victoria's home. Ancient elms gracefully lined both sides of the street, so tall their branches met in the middle. Their arching limbs created a tunnel of cool shade. Even though they were not everlastings, the light patterns and the overhead branches, so spellbound Tam that she tripped.

"Are you alright?" Victoria asked. Lost in the treetops, Tam did not answer. "People call our town an urban forest. Lovely, isn't it?"

Tam followed Victoria up three flag stone steps to the back door. As Victoria dug for her keys in her purse, Tam turned her attention to the house and yard.

Peeling paint, dead trees, brown lawn. This is a disaster! Worse than I ever saw when I was her charge. I have some gardening to do.

Yes we do! YOU were not looking at the time, said the fairy voice.

I was thinking only of myself. Tam plunked down both suitcases and looked over this dilapidated dwelling.

Rose and Pink were so delighted with Tam's willingness to serve; they grabbed hands and danced around and around.

Tam was surveying the damage. The once-manicured lawn had turned brown. The daisy bushes long since died; the camellias' shiny dark green leaves turned brittle; dried yellow chrysanthemums rattled in the breeze. Tam picked a faded flower and crumpled it between her fingers. Only the apricot tree was alive, watered by a kind neighbor. Although it had dropped its leaves for winter, the old mottled trunk still stood proud.

"We have some gardening to do," said Tam. Two swallow-tailed butterflies danced around the unseen fairies and Tam's head. Tam took them as a sign that new life was possible. Taking a long, slow deep breath, she tried to think positive. "This is a wonderful old house."

Fumbling for her keys, Victoria looked up at the leaves overflowing the gutters. She replied, "Yes, it WAS a long time ago. When I bought it, I planned on fixing it up. But Gabriel got sick, and all my money goes to his treatment." She opened the back door and yelled, "Gabriel, I'm home!" To Tam, she said, "He's usually lying on the living room couch. He has been sick for two years, so he has not been in school. I hope you don't mind."

"Mind?" said Tam. "Gabriel and I will be good friends."

"I hope so. Most of our friends don't like coming over because it makes them uncomfortable."

They passed through the kitchen, the counters were crammed with boxes and junk, the sink piled with dirty dishes, the old cereal pot still on the stove. Victoria's school papers were spread out at one end of the dining room table. At the other end, two ketchup-stained place mats and two dried milk glasses and two dried egg plates. An oak sideboard held several stacks of books that looked like they were about to fall over. Dust bunnies rolled along the oak floors as they walked by.

Victoria's husband had left them just after they learned Gabriel's diagnosis. He'd taken his car, his clothes, and his toothbrush; that was all, not even a suitcase. It was two weeks before Christmas. The next morning Victoria woke up, checked the garage and closets and computer. She had called his office, but they didn't know where he was. Not a note, not a phone call, not a word. She poured herself into creating a nice holiday for Gabriel. She never stopped to feel her shock or anger at his leaving; she never felt her dread over Gabriel's illness.

She hadn't shed a tear; she hadn't missed a day of teaching. Teaching kept her sane. The minute she said, good morning class, all her troubles vanished and she came alive. She loved her students and her son. When she walked home she fed Gabriel, tucked him in early, then she graded papers until the wee hours. She worked her students hard, but they loved her for it. Even though she'd been named Teacher of the Year, she didn't feel any joy. She was numb. She and Gabriel were surviving.

This is terrible! Her child is sick, her house is filthy, her garden is dead! She has no help, no family?

Rose answered, *"She is alone. Things are worse than the last time you were here."*

This will take a miracle! Tam said inwardly.

Gabriel lay on a worn-out plaid couch watching television.

"Gabriel, this is Tamara! She will be staying with us for a while...upstairs."

Gabriel said nothing; he just stared at the TV screen.

"I am sorry. We have not had guests for such a long time. He's forgotten his manners." Victoria took Gabriel's face in her hands and looked straight into his eyes. "Gabriel, don't be rude. Speak to our guest."

Gabriel said flatly, "Hi!"

"Hi, I am Tam." Tam pulled a card table chair close to the sofa. "What are you watching that is so captivating? What is that horrible high-pitched sound?"

Victoria shrugged her shoulders and said, "He watches television all day. I know he's not learning anything but at least he's occupied. I'm at school."

Tam thought, *He is pale, sick, and lonely.*

Rose said, *"How about playing some heavenly music?"*

Without saying another word, Tam walked over and turned the television off. "That's better," Tam said.

"Hey, what did you do that for?" Gabriel asked.

"Well," said Victoria, "I can see you two have some things to talk about. Tamara, I'd like to go to the store." They heard the back door shut.

Gabriel sat up and winced. He held his side and slumped down on the sofa and rested his head on the arm.

"Let us listen to something that brings joy." She turned on the music and the lovely sounds of Handel's Water Music filled the air. Tam let her body glide around the room to the music. She closed her eyes and let the heavenly sounds vibrate through her. When she opened her eyes, she saw Rose embracing Gabriel like a loving mother. Pink sat on the sofa back and placed one hand on Gabriel's head and the other on his side, where he complained of pain. When the music finished Tam sat down on the coffee table.

Tam hummed a little of the tune. Gabriel did not move or open his eyes. But he answered in a faraway voice: "I like that it is alive. It races like a stream. It..."

"Yes, exactly; and it is yellow and orange and red all at the same time," Tam shouted.

Rose and Pink motioned for Tam to keep her voice down. Pink said, "The loud noise strikes his painful body like small stones. Speak softly. Get him inside the music."

Tam nodded although she did not know how to do that. Grandmother Fairy had told her: When you are in service of another, you know the right thing to do.

Tam continued, "What colors did you see while the music was playing?"

"I saw blue and lavender swirls."

"Good! Now I will play it again.... And see those colors swirling all around you. .... As if the music itself were swirling around and through you."

Pink nodded and gave her a thumbs up. She rewound the tape and punched the play button. The music flooded the room. Gabriel's face relaxed and he sat up. Then Pink and Rose helped him to his feet. Although his eyes were still closed, Gabriel began slowly to move around the room, Pink on one side and Rose on the other. The threesome glided around the oak coffee table, passed the mantel, over and around the table that sat in the far window. Gabriel's arms seemed to float to the music; he moved a little faster now. If one looked very hard, one could even see lavender and blue swirling around the trio. As the music ended, Rose and Pink gently lead him back to the sofa. Gabriel opened his eyes looking much more alert.

"That was wonderful! Could you see the colors, Gabriel?"

"I felt the lavender and the blue going right through me. The music was liquid light that could... could travel inside me."

"Excellent, Gabriel. You are very advanced in your appreciation of music. Music is a heavenly vibration that you can get inside and heal you... Each one of us is tuned to a special vibration. Sometimes we go out of tune. This music can help you get back in tune."

"I never listened to music like that before." Gabriel's face seemed brighter.

"And music will never be the same after this, Gabriel. You will know the notes that are good for you because you will see them as colors. The music that is not good for you will hit your body like lead. Now, who wrote Handel's Water Music?"

"Handel, right?" Gabriel said. "How stupid can you be?"

"An angel wrote it for the Creator," Tam explained. "Then she played it on her celestial harp next to Handel's ear. He heard it so clearly, he could not write it down fast enough. Humans say he wrote it himself, but he had help." Gabriel just stared at her. "Do you know why it was written?"

He took a stab, "He wrote it for a king, I think."

"It was written to lift up the human spirit...Now let us listen to the whole piece together." Without hesitating Gabriel hit the play button and again the music flooded the room. This time Tam let the sounds vibrate through her while she danced around the room.

After the movement finished, Tam sighed, "That was magnificent! I am uplifted!"

Gabriel had tears in his eyes. Tam touched his arm, "It is hard to describe its beauty, isn't it? I am going to clean up around here."

After, Gabriel closed his eyes, and the fairies flooded him with green healing light flecked with energizing gold. The music's vibration opened his heart, so fairy love could enter and begin to heal him. Gabriel's pale cheeks glowed with a faint pink.

CHAPTER 9: THE CLEANUP

Standing at the kitchen sink, Tam asked, "Pink, Rose, do you do dishes?" Instantly, Rose shot the dishwater with red light.

Just then Gabriel appeared in the doorway. "Who were you talking to?"

"Oh, the dish fairies. I figure we could use all the help we can get. Perhaps we will not have to throw all these stinky dishes away and start over."

Gabriel pushed up his sleeves, grabbed the sponge and plunged his hands into the soapy water. Soon the drainer was stacked full, but Tam jumbled up the cups, and glasses and plates. As Gabriel washed, she started opening one cupboard and just piling the wet dishes on the shelves.

"Tam, Tam," Gabriel said firmly. "You have to dry them first. Didn't your mom teach you how to do dishes?" Tam shrugged her shoulders.

"You'd better show me how you do dishes at your house," Tam said sheepishly.

Gabriel opened a drawer, pulled out a fresh dish towel and wiped a glass dry. "Now, dry them first, we stack dinner plates here, then the smaller plates." He opened other cupboard, "Glasses go here, and cups hang on these little hooks," he pointed to the cup hooks underneath the cabinet.

"Kitchen Fundamentals! Thank you, Gabriel," and Tam went into action.

After doing more than he had done in months, Gabriel ran out of energy, pulled up a chair, and watched his new friend. Now, that she knew how the kitchen was arranged, Tam worked double time, so fast her body seemed to blur. She scoured the sink; scrubbed the floor; polished the stove. As she passed Gabriel, his mouth hung open in amazement. He thought he saw the sponge moving by itself. She swept the floor, dusted, and cleared the table. She stacked Victoria's papers in the rolltop desk and shut it. She came to a halt. She held out the broom and then leaned on it.

"That music gave me a lot of energy," said Tam.

"I'll say!" said Gabriel.

Just then Victoria walked into the kitchen. Her mouth fell open. She set down the grocery bags and leaned against the stove, and then gazed at the spotless counters and sparkling stove. "This is incredible!"

"You did this?" asked Victoria. For months he has not felt well enough to stand let alone help wash dishes.

Tam raised her eyebrows and shrugged her shoulders. "I had help from the dish fairies."

"Mom, I think she should stay."

"Why don't you two go outside while I fix us all a nice dinner. I bought chicken and pie for dessert." Victoria felt happy as she busied herself around the kitchen. Victoria cocked her head to one side and looked at him strangely pleased. "I don't know what's been going on around here, but I think I like it," she said.

Tam suggested, "Gabriel, let us go outside, if that is all right?"

CHAPTER 10: THE STORY

Gabriel grabbed two ragged beach towels. He led Tam through the hallway and out the front door to the one living thing in the yard, to the apricot tree. He spread out the towels and stretched out on the faded green one. Tam sat down letting her back rest against the tree and crossing her legs.

"Now, I would like to tell you a story. "This is a living story, a healing story, that is alive and is still being written," explained Tam.

"I'm a little big for stories." But he had nothing better to do, and he rather liked Tam.

Tam began to speak very slowly. Indeed, Gabriel closed his eyes. She had learned to slow herself down to listen to the wisdom of the trees while she was living with the elves. Now, she hoped she could slow Gabriel down so he would hear the truth in her message. Even if he fell asleep, she knew his deeper self would be listening.

"Once...upon ...a...time... far ... away... yet... just ... on... the... other... side... of... time... lived... a ... fairy."

Sitting in the apricot tree Rose and Pink listened closely: *What is she up to now?*

She continued to speak with that slow constant rhythm: "Once upon a time, there lived a fairy. She was not bad, but she did mean things ...sometimes. She talked back to her elders and fairies of rank; she broke fairy rules." Tam wondered if Gabriel was asleep.

She winked up at Rose and Pink and continued: "Even though she was rambunctious, she earned her right to watch over a human. But she was not ready; she was more interested in herself

47

than being of service. She did not appreciate the fairy gifts the Creator had given her.

"Because she did not practice Fairy Fundamentals, the Fairy Coach stripped her of her rank and took her wings. He banished her and told her she had to live among the elves.

"Now this fairy hated elves; they had green skin, and they were stupid. So, this was a horrible punishment. But perhaps the fairy way of doing things was not the only way. She realized that kindness and love were more important than even fairy gifts.

"After earning her wings back, the Great Fairy asked her to consider taking a new assignment: living as a human. This would help bring more light and joy to the humans who are suffering."

Tam put her hand on Gabriel's brow and stroked his head. She whispered in his left ear: "That fairy is here, Gabriel. We will get through this together. You have a big challenge, but you are up to it. The Creator only gives big jobs to big beings. I know." Rose knelt at Gabriel's feet and Pink stood behind Tam pouring a fine gold mist into Gabriel adding their strength and encouragement to her words.

CHAPTER 11: THE HEALING

During dinner Gabriel ate three pieces of chicken, two helpings of carrots, salad and pie. Victoria marveled at her son's appetite: "I have never seen you eat like that, Gabriel."

"I was hungry," he said stabbing another bite of apple pie with his fork.

"Mom, I must have slept while we were outside because I had the weirdest dream. While my body was still asleep, I stepped out of it. I saw a ball of rose-colored light was standing at my feet. It was saying something but I couldn't quite hear it. But we climbed up the apricot tree together just like I used to when I was little. Then we started somersaulting through the air. It was wonderful! I felt terrific!" He glanced at Tam who just smiled. "Then I had to come back to this...this sick body. And, I woke up."

Victoria had tears running down her eyes. "Mom, it was a happy dream!" He got up and hugged her around the neck. The tears were flooding down her face. She ran out of the dining room.

To Tam, he said, "I thought it would make her happy."

"It was a beautiful dream, very special." Tam got up and followed Victoria, but she had locked herself in the bathroom.

Pink and Rose melted through the door. Rose perched on the bathroom sink. Victoria was sitting on the throw rug, leaning against the cool tile wall, hugging her knees. She was weeping uncontrollably. Pink knelt behind her. As Victoria sobbed and sobbed, Rose pulled out the gray sorrow like endless scarves coming out of magician's hat. Then Pink cupped his hands together and a small ball of green light appeared. Pink put his palms over Victoria's heart, and the light sank into her.

After a few minutes, Victoria said, "I feel better." She stood up at the sink and splashed water on her face.

Rose said, "Pink, you've never done that before."

Pink answered, "The Creator heard my call, Victoria had a great need."

At the dining table Gabriel said, "I hear her crying at night when she thinks I am asleep. She thinks I am dying. Am I dying, Tam?"

Tam reached over and took Gabriel's hand, "I do not know. Only the Creator knows that. Are you afraid?"

"I don't know what it is like," he said.

"It is very much like your dream. You step out of your old sick body."

"If it is like that, then I am not afraid," Gabriel said. Tam put her arm around Gabriel's shoulder. After several minutes, Tam said gently, "I am right here with you; I am right here with you. We will walk through this together; we will walk through this together." Fairies always say this twice.

CHAPTER 12: FIRST DAY

Tam woke up to a muffled voice calling from downstairs: "Time to get up; it's your first day of school."

She had no wings, but Tam stretched with a series of fairy motions familiar to all fairies. She glanced down at the backyard. Everything was dead except a gnarled old sycamore tree. She could see the brick outline of the flowerbeds that remained even though the poppies, daisies, and geraniums had long since withered. No one had even bothered to pull off the dried flower heads.

"I am sorry, Creator, for not taking better care here. I can see I have some gardening to do. Outside sitting on the shingles a red robin -- about half the size of fairy's green robins -- sang.

"Good morning, robin. You are a small fellow," Tam said. He cocked his head as if he understood. "I have a friend like you in the Fairy Kingdom far away from here. Perhaps we can be friends too. It is going to be a great day. I can feel it." The robin took off and landed on a high sycamore branch. Tam sang:

> "Oh, dear robin,
> I wish I could fly,
> We could sail the skies.
> You and I, you and I.
> We could soar above the trees.
> Caressing every lovely breeze.
> Kissing the leaves.
> Hugging the clouds.
> I wish I could fly.

We could sail the skies.

You and I, you and I.

"My elf friend, Tanny, used to sing that. I know how she feels now."

Rose urged, "Come on, Tam, you will not being flying this morning. You have no time to dawdle or talk to the birds. The clock runs these humans' lives."

"Alright! Alright! I just felt so good after our work last night," Tam reflected.

Pink said, "Our real challenge will be those school children. Now, to the showers with you."

Tam hurried to the bathroom and turned on the ice-cold water full blast. She let the water cascade over her for a few minutes. She felt invigorated. After a quick dry, she leaped into today's outfit, blue walking shorts and top. She glanced down, and ...there was a new pair of white tennis shoes. She slipped them on and bounded down the stairs.

"Great day, Gabriel," she said as she sat down at the dining table.

He looked up from his cereal bowl and said, "Good morning, Tam."

Victoria walked in from the kitchen carrying her steaming coffee mug. Its strong aroma filled the dining room. The milk and orange juice cartons were already on the table.

Tam said, "Thanks for the shoes."

"I did not give you any shoes," said Victoria. Tam looked over at Rose and Pink perched on the oak sideboard and just shrugged their shoulders. "But you have to tie them; I have to tell that to my students all the time." Tam knelt and tied both shoe strings in knots.

Victoria, changing the subject, said, "Around here we are all pretty much on our own for breakfast. You fix whatever you want and wash your own dishes. You'll need to keep your room and the upstairs bathroom clean as well. OK?" Victoria took another gulp of her coffee.

"Yes, that is quite fine. I will do all the cleaning," offered Tam.

"Mom, she is very fast!"

"Are you sure? That's a huge job!" asked Victoria.

"Absolutely!" Tam drank down her juice, stood up and began clearing the table.

"Mom, she is here to help us!"

Tam finished putting the food away while Victoria finished her coffee. Then, she flew through the dishes. As Victoria walked her coffee mug into the kitchen, she caught a glimpse of Tam in double quick mode. The dishes almost looked like they were stacking themselves, but orderly this time. Dinner plates first, then smaller ones, mugs on the dish towel. Tam was drying her hands.

"See, mom; she's incredible!" He put his hand in his mom's shoulder.

"I'll say!"

Tam asked, "Gabriel, what advice can you give me for my first day?"

"Yes," Gabriel stared at Tam's shoes. "Tie your shoes properly. Are you from another planet?"

Victoria shouted, "Gabriel, be kind to our guest."

"I'm sorry, but really, Tam, don't you wear shoes?" And he knelt down and tied Tam's tennis shoes in double-knotted bows.

"Where I'm from, we went barefooted all the time," Tam said. "Thank you for the Shoe Fundamentals. Now, how about some Teacher Fundamentals?"

Gabriel leaned against the counter and thought. "Be firm, but have fun. Show and demand respect. I hope you don't get that Mitch kid."

"Gabriel, you'd think you were the teacher in this family."

"Good Teaching Fundamentals, I would say," said Tam.

"OK, time for all good teachers to get to school," Victoria announced kissing her son on the cheek.

"You will be alight alone?" asked Tam.

When Gabriel looked at her tight-lipped, she knew he did not like it, but he said, "I'll be fine! I feel better today."

"We will look in on him," whispered Rose.

Victoria picked up her briefcase and papers. Tam stood in a patch of sunlight warming her back while Victoria locked the door.

"Here's your house key," Victoria handed the key to Tam. "We keep an extra key under the first flower pot.

So many human rules to remember, Tam thought.

"By the end of today you'll have as much to carry and I do. You can use this." Victoria gave her a green and white striped canvas book bag.

And so much to carry! So much to carry!

When they were both on the sidewalk, Tam said, "You look brighter today." Victoria's smile told the whole story.

"I slept soundly for the first time in weeks. I only hope you don't get Mitch. He used to tease Gabriel unmercifully," said Victoria. "He set my trash can on fire last year, right in my classroom."

CHAPTER 13: THOMAS

As they walked onto the school grounds, Victoria called out to a custodian: "Thomas, this is Tamara Rupford. Could you open up her room for her? Miss Rupford, I'll see you at home after school. Good luck!"

Thomas grabbed a giant key ring off his belt. His khaki pants and navy blue T-shirt had paint splattered on them, but they smelled of laundry soap. He smiled that warm grin that so reminded Tam of the Fairy Coach.

"You must be very important," said Tam staring at his keys.

"Oh, yes! I have the key to everything!" He unlocked the door easily and held it open for her. "Where are you from?"

"Me? I am from a place where the flowers are always in bloom, where we live on light; where we live to serve," Tam said.

Thomas's face lighted up, "Sounds like the Creator has touched your life. Come with me, I want to show you something."

He took Tam by the elbow. She took two steps for each of his strides toward another building. Thomas pulled out his enormous key ring again and unlocked a metal gate.

"This is my wild garden. I don't show it to many people," he said. And he snapped open the pad lock and swung wide the gate. Tam beheld a tangled flower garden about 20 by 40 feet hidden right on the school grounds.

"Oh, my; oh, my," was all she could say. "Someone jumbled all the flowers up but it's wonderful."

"I did. This was just dirt when I started. The administration hasn't decided what to do with this land, so I tossed out packets of flower seeds, and let Nature do her thing. I've had fun identifying all these: coral bells, California poppies, prickly poppies, pink and yellow yarrow, blue-eyed grass, and purple strawflowers. I brought in those baby redwoods for shade from the botanical gardens right across the street. I know they're only 12 feet or so now, but they'll grow to be giants."

"Where I come from we call them everlastings," Tam said gazing up into their branches. Thomas had propped up his tools, rake, hoe, shovel, against the redwoods' trunks.

"Good name! They also gave me the rosemary and lavender too. These are all California natives, so they don't need much care. This is where I come to feel close to the Creator." Tam batted away a butterfly. "Those are painted lady butterflies; we only get them when we have a lot of rain." A swarm of them flitted around their heads.

Tam was dumbstruck. There were no paths or benches, just a riot of flowers. "Everything's all mixed up. Where I come from we plant each flower with its own kind," she said longing to touch the blossoms. "What are those?"

Tam lightly touched a plant with thin sword-like leaves; a thick stock was growing straight up its middle. At the end of the stock was a candle-shaped pod with orange tipped in yellow.

Thomas answered, "Those are called Indian paint brushes. I come here on my lunch hour to get away from it all."

"And these? I saw these purply fuzzy things at the train station."

Thomas said, "Those are wooly blue curls. I know they look purple. This garden gives me peace." He leaned up against an everlasting. "Mostly I plant flowers in their own beds too. But my mother and aunt taught me to leave a wild place like this for the fairies and elves."

Tam jerked her head around and stared at Thomas, "What? What did you say?" She was taken off guard.

"Fairies and elves. Don't you believe in them?"

"Well, yes, yes," Tam stuttered. "But what if you met...."

Thomas stooped to pull a weed not realizing the impact of his words. A bell rang, and he said, "Let's get you to class."

"I must come back. Please!" she managed to say.

"Yes, you can visit anytime," and Thomas padlocked the gate.

After a few long strides, Thomas propped open Room 813.

Tam stood gazing around the empty classroom, rows of desks, whiteboard, one large desk.

"I am scared, Thomas."

"Give the Creator your fear," suggested Thomas. Tam closed her eyes. Rose and Pink sprinkled a calming pale blue bath over both of them.

"That blue was beautiful!" blurted out Thomas. Tam's eyes flew open.

"You saw it?" she asked amazed.

"Yes. I see sometimes."

Tam said, "My grandmother told me some were beginning to see."

She took a position near the large desk; she took a deep breath, then another. She glanced down at her white knuckles gripping the tabletop. Her stomach was doing flip-flops. She closed her eyes and tried to let go and relax.

CHAPTER 14: THE TEACHING ASSIGNMENT

The bell rang, the door flew open and in marched her students. One young man in jeans and a white T-shirt slumped into the last desk. Another similarly dressed slammed his books down on a desk and sat down. A girl in shorts and a plaid flannel shirt followed and flopped in a front seat. She began combing her heavy, long brown hair. Her bubble gum snapped as she chatted with another girl who sat down right behind her. Tam was fascinated that the girl could chew the stuff and talk at the same time.

"Hey, teach," the girl with the long brown hair said. "We ran off the last substitute! Let's see how long you last."

"I will probably out last you!" Tam answered planting her feet firmly on the floor and putting her hands on her hips. "In this class you will show respect. Now, you cannot think and chew that stuff at the same time. So please get rid of it."

Carmen raised her eyebrows a little surprised that this new teacher took control so quickly. She put her gum in a tissue and put it in her purse.

"I'll bet she can't think at all," said the boy across the room. Carmen's face clouded over.

Tam stepped toward the boy. "Yes, what is your name?"

"Mitch!" He puffed out his chest.

"Mitch, we respect all being in this class. You'll be respectful to me, Carmen and all of us. Now, please apologize to Carmen for your remark," Tam said.

"I didn't mean it; she knows I was just fooling around," Mitch replied.

Tam continued, "Fooling around or not, you hurt people with your words.... Now say I am sorry." Mitch paused to see if she was serious. Tam did not back down; in fact she began moving toward Mitch.

"I'M SORRY, OK?" Mitch glared.

The girl near Tam's desk started combing her hair. Then she tossed her head so it brushed the boy behind her.

The boy jumped out of his seat, his jaw tightened, and shouted, "Stop that! ... Teacher!" The girl was out of her seat her fists clinched. Rose flew between them in a fairy flash. Pink had the boy by the shoulders.

Tam yelled, "Sit down immediately." Tam's eyes got round as saucers. She took another breath and regained her composure.

"You are going to fight because she accidentally hit you with her hair? If you are going to do battle, let it be over something big. ... And then fight to win. Fighting with your fists, you never win." She turned to the girl. "What is your name?"

"Laurel! And that's Howie."

"Laurel, put the comb away. No grooming in my class. Besides you are beautiful already."

Tam walked back to the front of the room and turned to face her class. "Now, that I have passed your little tests!" She beamed and her students returned her smile. Everyone relaxed. "Good! Let us begin.... I am Tam...Tamara Rupford. Miss Rupford.... Where I come from we greet each other. Stand up please one at a time and tell me your name." She made each student -- Mitch, Howie,

Carmen, Laurel, the boy who had had his head down, all of them --
stand and shake her hand.

By now, Pink had retreated to the pencil sharpener. He
managed to say, *The wing smoke in here is very thick, Rose.*

Rose sat on a dictionary with her knees drawn up to her chest.

*Pink, I hear that some young humans even like hanging onto
angry feelings and then, if you can believe this, they enjoy spraying
them at others.*

What can we do, Rosie?

Mitch raised his hand and said, "I failed all my classes last
semester. I don't think you'll be able to teach me anything."

"You sound proud of that fact. I would be ashamed. You are
bright and pretending not to be. We must use our gifts or they are
taken away. I know all to well, Mitch."

"Miss Rumpford, with respect, how do you know?"

Tam gave a quick look at Rose and Pink. "Well, perhaps I will
tell you, but not today."

Then Laurel raised her hand and stated: "This is the dumb
class. They put us here while they are figuring out how to get rid of
us."

Tam walked right up to Laurel's desk, "Let us prove them
wrong. I am not getting rid of anyone. I know you can succeed.
Everyone in here can succeed. I know it!" She said it so boldly they
were intrigued. She slapped her hand on the desk, and Laurel
jumped. "Now, here is your first assignment: I am from another
kingdom...."

One student blurted out: "Like ET!"

A girl asked, "What is that?"

"An extraterrestrial, stupid! A creature from another planet," answered the boy.

"WE MUST SHOW RESPECT AT ALL TIMES! That is our first Classroom Fundamental," Tam announced as she wrote it on the white board in big blue letters. "Come write these down on the board for us... in your best handwriting." Tam walked down the row and handed Mitch the board pen.

"I don't write too good," Mitch admitted.

"Yes you will. When you have a bigger purpose, you do your best work... Come now," Tam urged. And Mitch wrote in big block letters:

SHOW RESPECT TO ALL.

NO JUDGING.

"Now, what other rules would you have in your classroom?" Tam asked. And the students came up with this list:

BE FAIR.

ONE AT A TIME.

NO THROWING THINGS.

Then Tam said, "I would like to add: DO YOUR BEST! NO BLAMING OTHERS.

"My little sister is always blaming me," said Carmen. "How many of you have blamed another?" Several hands went up.

Then Tam declared, "If your hand is not up, I bet you are lying." The students laughed. "I know I am right because I used to do the same thing." *She is very out spoken, she makes a good human.* Pink pointed out. Pink slipped his arm into Rose's; they beamed at their charge. If one were a fairy one could see, they both flexed their feet in their new white tennies.

Then Rose whispered, *These shoe things are not too bad as long as I do not have to walk. Perhaps I could get a rose colored pair.*

Oh, Rose, you are thinking like a fairy. We need to think like humans. Rose jumped up and began pacing up and down the bookcase stepping carefully over the dictionaries.

Perhaps if I use my feet like a human, I will have human thoughts. And Pink began prancing along the chalk rail.

Ms. Rupford said, "We are going gardening tomorrow."

"That's boring!" said Howie.

"I promise you this class will I never be boring. I love gardens and flowers. Besides, there is someone who needs our help. He just lives a few blocks from here. He cannot come to school, so we will take class to him. You will get an A for the day if you bring a hoe, or a rake, or a shovel."

One very shy, skinny girl said, "I have never gotten an A."

"You will tomorrow, and you will learn and have fun. I promise!" Tam proclaimed with a broad grin on her face. The bell rang, and the students ran out joining the sea of youngsters finding their way to their next class.

Tam flopped into the teacher's chair. "That was work! They were ... well, I cannot begin to describe them. Was I ever that bad?"

"Worse!" declared Rose and Tam rolled her eyes.

The skinny shy girl poked her head in the door and said, "Who are you talking to, Miss Rupford?" She was twisting her tan sweater.

"Oh, no one. I did not get your name."

"Evelyn, but people call me Evie.... I.... I just wanted you to know I like your class. Those kids were horrible to you and you handled them very well. No teacher ever gets Mitch to do any work."

"Thank you, Evie. Thank you very much," Tam stood up and smiled although she was tired from the workout her students had given her.

As Evie turned to go, Rose and Pink threw some pink sparkles at her. "That one needs lots of love," Rose said.

"And Tam you need to thank your fairy helpers," demanded Pink acting very human-like. Pink stood his full height and thrust his hands straight up in the air.

"Yes, thank you both very much! I could not he done it without you." She kicked off her tennis shoes and collapsed again in her chair.

Rose added, "Good Fairy Fundamentals, I would say, Tam."

"I am glad you noticed. I am very glad you are both here." Rose and Pink floated over to Tam's chair and hugged their charge warmly.

CHAPTER 15: MR. MATTHEWS

As soon as Tam was off the school grounds, she shouted, "Hurray! I made it through the first day!" Rose did two somersaults through the air, then several aerial spirals. Pink zoomed to a treetop, shot back down, whirled around Tam, and shot back up to the elm tree.

Tam stopped a moment. "I wish I could fly with you." Her wing attachments ached. Rose and Pink eased down to the ground and floated along side her a few inches off the ground.

"We will walk with you," Pink said putting his arm around Tam's shoulders.

"Today you have been of great service to those young humans. The light is stronger in your students. That is more thrilling than any somersaults in the air," said Rose.

"I hope so!" said Tam.

"I know so! I know so!" Rose repeated as all Fairies on Assignments do.

The three rounded the corner onto Victoria's block. Across the street children on the merry-go-round whirled faster and faster as their happy screams rippled through the park. A mother walked close behind her toddler who was taking tentative steps on the grass. One girl pumped her feet to get her swing as high as she could. Six small ones splashed wildly in the wading pool.

But Tam's eyes focused on a lush rose garden next door to Victoria's house, dozens of carefully pruned bushes. Tam hopped onto the low brick wall to drink in the rose scent.. There along the side of this slate blue cottage were roses: deep red, orange, buttery yellow, lemon yellow, pale ivory, lavender. The miniature pink climbing roses that wound around a white trellis framed the entrance to the garden. Not a leaf on the manicured lawn; not a withered blossom on the dozens of rosebushes, a well-tended garden.

"I know fairies in every one of these colors," said Tam aloud. She picked an orange one, closed her eyes, and let the smell and color vibrate through her.

"What are you doing? You are stealing my roses!!" a voice thundered.

Her eyes flew open, and a man roared out his screen door waving his arms. Tam dropped the precious bloom and began to run. But Rose and Pink grabbed her by the shoulders.

"Ask his permission. Humans think flowers belong to them."

"Everyone knows flowers belong to the Creator," Tam exclaimed. The fairies' touch calmed her.

"Tam, we are in the human realm, we have to abide by human customs," said Rose.

So Tam summoned her courage and turned to face the man. He was walking among his roses talking to them as if they were small children. "My beauties," he cooed.

"I am Tamara Rupford," she interrupted. "I live across the street with
Victoria and Gabriel."

"You were stealing my prize roses. I am Sylvester Matthews, Mr. Matthews to you. I work hard all year to grow these beauties." He glared at Tam.

"Yes, I can see that. I was just appreciating them. And in winter, they are blooming in winter. You must be working with the Creator's magic."

Mr. Matthews stuck his callused hands in the bib of his navy overalls. "Well, Miss, I don't know about that. I was a biology teacher at the high school. Now that I am retired I spend most of my time in this garden."

Since Beatrice, his wife of 35 years, had died, he kept the place immaculate inside and out. He'd just finished painting two white Adirondack chairs in the garden where they used to sit and have morning coffee. The two white wicker chairs on the front porch had new flowered chintz seat cushions. He kept the last book she was reading on a wicker side table. Beatrice had been re-reading Alice in Wonderland for the umpteenth time. She loved children's literature. His need for order kept his sadness away.

Inside, not a dirty dish in sight; his science magazines and newspapers stacked neatly. No dirt would dare enter Sylvester Matthew's house. Beatrice's picture in its brass frame sat properly on the mantle. Before he went to bed each night he stopped at her picture and touched it tenderly. Perhaps if he kept it all just as she had, she might come waltzing through the door.

Mr. Matthews sneezed, automatically pulled out a red bandanna handkerchief, and blew his nose. He sneezed again, and blew so loud Tam stepped back.

"Hay fever," Mr. Matthews complained. "I love to grow flowers, but the pollen makes my sinuses..." He dabbed his watery eyes with the hanky, and blew his reddened nose again. The honking sound made Tam want to laugh but she didn't.

What can we do for him? He is obviously suffering! Tam said inwardly.

Instantly, Rose and Pink rushed to Sylvester Matthew's side. While they hovered over him, they flooded him with green. Rose took silver threads and wove them around his head. Then both fairies floated over to the roof so they could observe their handiwork.

Tam continued as if nothing unusual had happened. "I am a teacher also. I have some unusual...well, challenging students. And... I would like to use some of your roses in my lesson."

"Why didn't you say so!" Mr. Matthews stuffed his bandanna into the front pocket of his overalls. He took two sniffs through his nose. "Funny!
My nose just opened up. I can breathe again!" Rose and Pink motioned her to remain silent.

Mr. Matthews went on, "I am always glad to help a fellow teacher. I taught for 29 years. What are you teaching?"

"Mr. Matthews, I am teaching them to do their best, to experience life, to be loving."

He raised his bushy eyebrows and gives a quick grin. "What subject is that?"

"Life!" replied Tam.

Mr. Matthews did not know quite what to say, so he merely said, "Yes. How many roses do you need?"

"I would like one for each student, Mr. Matthews."

"Any specific color?"

"No! All colors!"

"I'll just go and get my garden shears." Sylvester Matthews walked into the shed. Tam smiled up at her helpers; they gave her a thumbs up letting their feet dangle over the rain gutter. While Tam waited, she smelled a peach rose taking in its rich color. She could have stayed there all day.

"These roses remind me of the Rose Pool in the Great Fairy's garden. She closed her eyes and, just for a moment, pictured her fairy home.

CHAPTER 16: THE ROSE POOL

No one knew exactly where the Great Fairy lived, but fairies did know she lived near the Rose Pool. No fairy ventured to the pool without invitation, so all eagerly awaited the Rose Pool Ceremony.

At the far end of the pool a trumpet swan flapped his enormous wings and glided to a landing near his mate. The two drifted slowly as a gentle waterfall sent out a fine mist. Its quiet rush blended with the breeze that swayed the everlastings.

Legend said that the Great Fairy used her power to manifest whatever flowers she desired. Different flowers were blooming every time fairies came to the Rose Ceremony. Last time the pool gardens were covered in rockroses. Today crocuses bloomed in yellow, blue and purple while light and dark pink peonies clustered around the rocks. Bearded iris – blues, bronzes and yellows -- hugged the tree trunks. Between the rocks grew watercress and spearmint. And always, ever-blooming roses in every fairy color including shades not yet discovered in other realms. Only a few high ranking fairies, the Great Fairy being one of them, knew that fairy gardening planted the seeds for love in the human world.

The fairies gathered around the flat shale rocks that surrounded the pool. They arranged themselves by color: reds, oranges, yellows, greens, blues, and purples. Within each color were endless shades and hues: lavender, mauve, magenta, vermilion, peach, saffron, emerald, indigo, fuchsia. The rainbow was a wondrous sight for any being to behold. Everyone attended except young fairies that still were their primary colors.

The Rose Pool Ceremony took place when two or more demonstrated their maturity and dedication. Unlike the annual Dance of the Fireflies that sent the new Fairies on Assignment on their way, this was a more personal gathering. At the Rose Pool, the Great Fairy set each of her subjects on his or her path.

This morning the Great Fairy hovered over the highest rock, her wings without number fanned out behind her. Red stood on her left, Yellow at her right. She began as she always did: "Good day, fairies!"

"Good day to you," muttered thousands of fairies.

"Today these two take a step closer to fulfilling the Creator's plan." Then she handed Red and Yellow a pure white rose. "Red, dip your rose into the Pool and see the color of your destiny." Her voice rang out over the rushing falls.

Red knelt down and dipped his white rose holding onto its stem. Trembling with anticipation, Red lifted out the flower. He gave a gentle gasp. It had turned a deep color.

"Garnet!" the Great Fairy announced. A great flutter was heard throughout the assembly. Then Yellow dipped her rose, waited a few moments, pulled it out, and held it high for all to see.

"Lemon!" announced the Great Fairy. Then she handed each a crystal goblet filled with water from the pool. The goblets were carved with ancient designs but clear so everyone could see their liquid. The Great Fairy turned to Red first. He put his rose in the goblet. It melted into liquid garnet. The Great Fairy lifted the vessel high for all to see, and then held it so Red could drink. As he did, his wings turned a deep garnet. They shimmered and shook a few moments as they tuned to their finer vibration. The Great Fairy placed her hands on his head:

"I bless thee Garnet in the name of the Creator. From this day on this divine creature will be known throughout the realms as Garnet."

Now Yellow tenderly placed her rose in her goblet and let it melt. Assisted by the Great Fairy she drank the magic liquid slowly. As she did her wings turned the color of her destiny, Lemon.

"I bless thee Lemon," the Great Fairy's voice resounded again. As she put her hand on Lemon's head she continued, "From this day forth, this divine creature will be known as Lemon."

"Today we witness another of the Creator's miracles. These two are now ready for a human observation day. Fairy Coach?"

From behind the crowd, The Fairy Coach flew forward. "Yes, Great Fairy, I am here!" He bowed his head.

"Do we have a Fairy on Assignment who could use some additional assistance? Something where these young ones can see fairies interacting with humans."

He thought a moment surveying the multitude of fairies and said, "Yes, indeed! I believe we do!"

"Good! Let us send Lemon and Garnet, of course, and Vermilion, and Lime." As she announced these names, her sphere of golden light enveloped her. She rose up, her wings without number trailing behind her and glided over to each touching them lightly on the head. While her wings began to fold into an elegant train, she turned toward the waterfall.

Her form started shimmering and fading slowly getting smaller and smaller until it was an iridescent point of light. With every fairy watching, she light merged into the waterfall. She was gone.

CHAPTER 17: THE ROSE LESSON

Tam was loaded down with roses and papers. Her left hand held a huge bouquet of Mr. Matthews' roses, the stems wrapped carefully in wet paper towels; her right hand held a canvas bag bulging with papers. Managing to get one hand free, she fumbled for her keys. With all the jostling, one pink rose dropped on the cement.

Just then, Evie ran up. "Miss Rupford, let me help you open your room." Evie knelt down and gently picked up the bloom while Tam struggled unlocked the door.

"Thank you, Evie. I do not know if I could have managed without you." Evie gave a shy smile looking out from under her bangs. She held the door open while Tam walked inside.

"What are all the flowers for?"

"Evie, we are going on an adventure! And these roses will be our guides." Evie set her books down as Tam dropped her bag at her desk.

"They need water right away, Miss Rupford.... Do you have a vase?" Evie's eyes scouted the shelves.

"No!" said Tam. "Do they need one?"

"Roses will wilt if they don't get water fast. My grandma had beautiful roses, she taught me that."

Thank goodness for Grandma! Tam thought.

"Miss Rupford, I'll go to the office and ask Mrs. Wagner for a vase. She always has flowers on her desk." Evie bounded out the door happy to be useful.

The bell rang and Tam's rag-a-muffin class sauntered in. As Tam smiled at her students, she had them lined up their garden tools behind her desk. She said to herself,

We will create such magic today that they will all want to come to class. But as she glanced around at the plain cement block walls, she began to doubt.

Rose, who was observing from the pencil sharpener, said, *"Tam, everything you need is inside you, everything you need is inside you."*

YOU can create an entire Universe within these walls, Pink reassured her. *WE know our worlds are as real as this one. Your students only know what they see with their eyes open. Today you will open them to new kingdoms.*

Tam did not quite hear the last of Pink's words. She was focused on her students. The final bell rang and Tam, Miss Rupford, began: "Good morning, we will be going gardening tomorrow. Today, we are going to do inner gardening. Good morning, Mitch!" He just stared at her in silence. Tam slapped a book on her desk.

The class jumped and Mitch blurted out, "Good morning, Miss Rupford."

"Exactly! It is a good morning!" Miss Rupford replied completely in charge.   She walked down the aisle to Laurel's desk.

"Good morning, Miss Rupford!" Laurel tossed her long brown hair but this time she didn't hit anyone.

"Exactly! Our words make it so. We say it is a good morning, and it is. That is the power to create. ... Good Morning, Carmen." Miss Rupford made each and every student greet her clearly and confidently. She had seen the Fairy Coach do this with fairies in training a thousand times. Before she thought he was just flexing his authority. Now Tam understood how such a simple exercise could be a training tool. In three minutes she had them following directions, her directions. And, she had them practicing the Fairy Fundamental: WE CREATE OUR OWN LIVES.

Just then Evie walked in with a vase brimming with water. As she passed Mitch's desk, he stuck his foot out. Evie started to trip, but Rose flew over and caught her by the elbow. The students only saw that Evie recovered her balance without spilling a drop.

"Thank you, Evie!" Miss Rupford announced. "I only send special students on errands." Evie smiled. "Mitch, stand immediately!... For being cruel and hurtful you will not participate in our class today, and you will not get to go on our field trip." She paused to let her words sink in. "To the office..." She pointed toward the door.

Pink whispered in Tam's ear, "Someone gave you another chance." Tam smiled.

"Mitch, what Fairy Fundamental do you need to practice?" Flustered Tam corrected herself: "I mean what student fundamental?" Mitch looked confused.

But Howie said, "Respect."

"Yes, respect! Everyone deserves respect!" Perhaps Mitch understood now.

"Remember that and you can go with us," Tam said.

"Oh, thank you Miss Rupford." Mitch brightened. "No one has ever given me a second chance."

Tam shifted to mood. "Now, we are in for a treat." She held the vase smelling its perfume.

Everyone wanted to know: What are they for? Who are they from? A boyfriend?

"No, students, they are part of our lesson today. Sylvester Matthews gave them to us."

Howie burst out: "Old man Matthews! Yuck!"

Tam raised her free hand and pointed to Howie, "We show respect at all times...Yes! I know! He can be cranky! But he gave each one of you a rose... One of his prize roses. I think he must be lonely." Tam set the roses on her desk.

"Miss Rupford, could I have the pink one?" asked Evie.

"Maybe. Today the roses will select you; its color will be the color of your destiny." The class looked puzzled but interested. Tam did not care if they understood, she just wanted their undivided attention. And, she had it; they were all staring at her.

She began: "Now, put your heads down and close your eyes." Amazingly, every student followed her direction. Tam glanced over at Rose.

Where is Pink? Rose shrugged her shoulders. Then, Tam closed her eyes: *Let these young humans see what is possible for them. And, Creator, I could use some help.*

When Tam opened her eyes, she could hardly believe.... Their presence gave the gray cement block room a strange look. She started to exclaim, but Pink rushed up to silence her. Tam's heart jumped for joy. Her gray classroom had a familiar glow and a familiar hum. She wanted to run and skip and turned cartwheels all at once. There lined up along the back wall were...

Pink whispered in Tam's left ear, *"Begin your lesson, Miss Rupford!"*

Tam felt warm peace and excitement she felt when she saw the Great Fairy or when she had been with the Inneis, the Head Elf. For a fairy flash her mind was blank, words seemed far away. She drew in a long, deep breath... and then another just as the head elf, the Inneis, had taught her. Then, she heard her Great Grandmother Fairy's words in her head:

"Now, students, breathe...."

Tam answered back inwardly, *Oh, Grandmother, I miss....*

This is not about you. You asked for help and it is here. Just quiet your mind, and let my words come through you.

Tam's voice spoke softly and rhythmically: "Now, students take a long deep breath and let yourself relax. ... Now imagine you are in a special place... a place that is perfect for you ... see it in color, feel the sun, smell the fresh air.... In front of you is a perfect rose ... The rose is the perfect color for you. It has been picked for your inner garden. That rose has chosen you.... It is a magic rose. It can help you become what you are destined to be."

Pink motioned for Tam to be silent. She just smiled and beheld the fairies lined up along the back wall. One by one each fairy flew up to the bouquet. First, Vermilion glided forward and lifted out the rose of his shade. Pink pointed him to Howie, and Vermilion moved to his desk and placed the Vermilion rose near Howie's face. Vermilion hovered overhead. Then, Lemon came up and picked the lemon rose. She moved over to Evie's desk placing her rose near Evie. Now, Lime took the white rose and moved toward his student. Garnet selected the rose of his hue and found his assigned student. And so it continued until each student had an invisible helper and a very visible rose. Their fairy presence shimmered even against the dull cement block.

Filled with awe and appreciation, Tam observed silently. Her mind began to fill with words again: "When you take this next breath you will smell roses. Now breathe in.... deeply.... good.... Let that fragrance fill your being with joy and comfort and peace.... Good! Sit up straight and put your hands out as if to receive a special present."

Without a sound each fairy placed a rose in each student's open hand. A smile graced the lips of the humans, and the visiting fairies took their positions... on the left shoulder, of course. Evie, looking a little sleepy, opened he eyes and said, "I knew my rose was yellow! I could see it!"

"Good Evie, you can see with your inner eyes," said Tam.

No one else spoke; they just stared spellbound at their precious gift.

Now what do I do! Tam thought. And Pink pulled on his ear signaling her to listen, listen inwardly. Again, can heard Grandmother fairies voice:

"Look at your roses with great love ... as if it were a small child. Explore every petal. Notice how some petals look darker, some lighter. Some are tipped with another shade. ... Close your eyes. And smell your rose's fragrance. Pretend you can let its color with all its hues and shades vibrate through you. It gives you a deep sense of peace and calm. It is giving you exactly what you need right now, a connection to all that is.

"Now imagine you can make yourself very small ... so small you can fit inside your rose." At that moment each fairy placed a loving hand on each student's head. "In this rose chamber your being filled with goodness and love. You are successful and bright and capable. You know you can do your schoolwork easily, you know you can handle what life has in store for you. ... You know you are loved deeply and forever. You know you are loved deeply and forever."

Tam stood spellbound watching this very magic. She had witnessed hundreds of fairies whispering their words to humans. But she had never been right in the middle of ... well, human life.

What do I do now, Grandmother?

There was no answer, but somehow she knew. Tam walked to the closet and brought out paper and crayons. She said softly, "Now, students, open your eyes. Take paper and colors; draw what you saw. No one moved. She glanced at the fairies for help. Rose, Pink, Lemon, all of them held up two fingers.

Just like any good fairy on assignment Tam repeated her instructions twice: "Now students, open your eyes. Now students, open your eyes." She clapped her hands together hard. Several pairs of eyes popped open. "Good. Take paper and colors and draw what you experienced. Take paper and colors and draw what you experienced. "

Carmen got up and walked to Tam's desk and got her supplies. Mitch, very sleepy but moving, selected several crayons and paper. In a few minutes they were all drawing and drawing silently.

After a while Tam walked carefully over to Mitch's desk and watched his drawing take shape. She did not want to disturb him. An exquisite rose blossom brimming with life and detail was emerging on his paper. This rough young man had a delicate and artistic hand. Tam gently placed her hand on Mitch's left shoulder and said softly, "I feel I am right face to face with the rose in your drawing."

Mitch never looked up or stopped fleshing out his sketch. "That is just the way I saw it. ... well, I didn't see it really. ... I was there, in it." He turned his neck and looked straight into Tam's eyes. "Miss Rupford, do you know what I mean?"

"Yes, yes, I do! Indeed I do!"

Tam moved toward Evie who still had her eyes closed. "Evie where are you?"

"I'm floating in the most delicious yellow!"

"Good!" Tam smiled at Lemon who was hugging Evie about her neck.   "Evie, stay there as long as you like." Evie put her head down again and returned to dreaming.

Tam realized that the love pouring into these humans was far more important than their drawings. And Evie was swimming in it. Tam looked at each student; they looked softer, lighter, and indeed they were. Tam stood at the back of room and said silently:

Creator, I have witnessed one of your miracles again today. These humans have received your love ... deeply. We fairies will keep it alive. These humans had forgotten. We will remind them. They are loved. They are not alone.

Tam was filled with such joy she had a hard time finding the words to say, "Class dismissed!"

Her students filed out quietly, all but Evie who was still sleeping. Tam realized the girl must be dreaming. Tam took the few steps to Evie's desk and tapped gingerly on her left shoulder, then tapped again. Evie stirred and slowly opened her eyes. Two tears were rolling down her flushed cheeks.

With all the tenderness of Grandmother Fairy, Tam began, "Evie, you can take your rose home and put it by your bed. Ask to dream about her. See what she has to teach you."

Still groggy, still sounding very far away, Evie replied, "Miss Rupford, I was walking through a garden with low box hedges in curvy patterns like the labyrinth at the depot. Right in the garden center, I saw a giant rose shimmering white with silvery gold edges. It seemed to be shaking, no, I think it was breathing. It was inviting me closer. I walked into a warm 'softly-ness.' There was more love than I have ever felt in my life."

Tears flowed freely down Tam face, "And you still feel it?"

"Yes! Oh, yes! "

"Good, that is truly a blessing. You will feel that love for a long time!"

Tam and Evie closed their eyes and let the wonder of this rose lesson wash over them. Pink and Rose flew over and with their fairy wings embraced them both.

CHAPTER 18: THE PLAIN BROWN WRAPPER

Tam was so excited. If she had been in her fairy body, she would have shot straight up to the treetops and triple spiral spins and aerial zigzags around the clouds. Instead when she got to the park, she did four somersaults for shear joy.

Then she ran up the brick path and through the white trellis, she yelled, "Mr. Matthews, Mr. Matthews!" Out of breath, she shouted, "What a day! The class. I mean the roses. They were the stars, the flowers I mean… it was."

"In here, in the greenhouse," a muffled Mr. Matthews replied.

Tam followed his voice, opened the door just to the side of the garage and stepped into a small greenhouse. Damp heavy air hit her in the face.

A voice shouted, "Close the door immediately! These plants need climate control!"

Tam felt she was stepping into another world. She saw huge hanging begonias in the oranges, pinks and reds. The pinks were ruffly doubles. Tall bunch palms stood in the corners surrounded by containers of orchids. Tam had never seen these purple, white and yellow-green tropical plants. She eyed the tiny yellow mini orchids with orange dots. Broad leafed vines twisted up to the ceiling.

Trays of seedlings just a few inches tall sat on warming tables. Tam's feet crunched on the pea gravel as she stepped closer to the tables to read the carefully lettered labels: green beans, snow peas, cherry tomatoes, sweet peas, seedless watermelons and more. Against the back wall, a small fountain; a wind god spitting water.

"Mr. Matthews, the roses! What a class!"

"Slow down, girl! You're talking all jumbled up." Sylvester Matthew's popped his head up from behind his hanging baskets. "Slow down. Tell me everything." He continued to water.

"Mr. Matthews, are you listening? Respectfully, Mr. Matthews, could you look at me? I need to know if you are listening."

He darted a quick glance in Tam's direction and went back to his flowers. But in that glance Tam saw through the tough old man. Something inside her melted. She stepped closer resting her hand on his left shoulder.

"You love your flowers?" Tam asked gently.

"Yes, very much," replied Mr. Matthews. He was still staring at his begonias. He sat down his watering can and put his hands deep inside his pockets.

Very gingerly Tam asked, "Do you love anything… anyone else?"

"Yes, once a long time ago! My Beatrice is gone; now I am alone." The lines on his face deepened before Tam's eyes.

The Beatrice of the roses. Of course! thought Tam

"No, you are not alone at all." Tam put her hands on her hips and planted her feet firmly on the ground. Something in her was determined. When Sylvester Matthew's eyes filled with tears, Tam softened. She began:

"I see you I see you

Fighting with yourself, there.

I was once like that, so alone

 I see you, I see you,

I know you care.

87

You are love in plain brown wrapper.

"Sometimes where I live, used to live, we sing, and the singing teaches us something the heart needs to learn:

"You are love in a plain brown wrapper

I see you, I see you

Hiding under there.

I see you I see you

So wanting to care.

I know you, I know you.

I was once like you

I so, I so wanted

So wanted to share.

Tam took his callused hand in hers.

"Now close your eyes. Tell me, tell me what would life be like if you could care?"

The tears were streaming down Mr. Matthews's face now. He started to run into the house. Tam quickly looked around for Pink and Rose, then she shouted: "NO! You cannot run away!

"I know you, I know you

This is your chance; this is your chance,

I know you're scared.

But if you dare

To take off that brown wrapper

I guarantee… a life beyond compare.

So please, take off that brown wrapper

Come back, come back and share.

I see you, I see you hiding over there."

Sylvester Matthews pulled out his red bandanna and blew his nose. Then he turned on the worn heels of his old work boots and marched out of the greenhouse. The door slammed. Tam heard his back door slammed shut a moment later.

Inwardly Tam said, *I know he has loving heart; I can feel that, very faint, but I can feel it.*

Tam covered her face with her hands. She began to rock back and forth like a fairy in distress. Her wing attachments ached. "I have violated the First Fairy Fundamental: Do No More Harm Than Is Already Being Done."

Before Tam could finish her thoughts, Rose and Pink rushed to her side. Each fairy took a hand and gently pulled them from Tam's face. Tam's face was flushed with frustration.

Rose began, "I disagree!" Indeed, it was the first time Rose had ever disagreed with anything or anyone. But these were changing times that required even fairies to change. "You do not know if you have harmed him. This human has hardened his heart to love. You demonstrated the Tenth Fairy Fundamental: Love Unconditionally!" Tam was staring straight at Rose now. Gold and silver strands were winding themselves around Tam.

Pink added, "You even demonstrated the very challenging Eleven Fairy Fundamental."

"Really?" Tam said softly. "You mean I found a way to Love the Unlovable?"

"Yes!" They both declared simultaneously. These fairies gently guided Tam each taking one of her elbows. "Now let us go home."

Crossing the street to Victoria's house, Tam said, "I so want Mr. Matthews to know he is loved again."

"A human heart that has turned to stone is most difficult," stated Pink. "But we will find a way, we will find a way," said the fairies.

CHAPTER 19: A BALL OF LIGHT

Soon after Tam left, Sylvester Matthews flopped onto his green overstuffed chair. He barely managed to pull the afghan Beatrice had crocheted -- green, blue, orange, and yellow squares with brown edging -- around him, and then he fell into a deep sleep.

Pink found him snoring softly. He fluttered midair just in front of the chair.

"Creator, if this is the time of healing for Sylvester Matthews, let me know the way; if it be thy will, let me be the vessel."

A moment later Pink saw what looked like translucent dirt clods coming out of Sylvester Matthews' chest. There were dozens of these dried up old lumps of energy ready to be pulled out. Pink's work took several minutes.

As Pink pulled them out, he remarked, "No wonder you felt so miserable!"

All the clods collected into misty magenta light just above Pink's head, and disappeared. Pink cupped his hands and closed his eyes asking again for assistance. A ball of red light appeared in his palms. He quickly placed them over Sylvester Matthews' chest. The light jumped into his heart.

Pink thought, *Thank your Creator for the privilege of helping this man.*

He said softly, "You will feel better now."

CHAPTER 20: COLOR TRAINING

A light breeze blew through the Fairy Kingdom swaying the boughs of the everlastings. As the sun rose, young fairies were sliding down sunbeams letting the sun's rays energize them.   Their wings – red, orange, yellow, green, blue and purple – turned the sunshine into beams of shimmering colors, dazzling rainbows. When the sun rose higher and the morning mist burned off, they dashed to the river and danced on the waters' diamonds. Fairies loved the game of flitting and prancing with the prisms of light as the water reflected the sun. As they grew older there would be less time for flitting down sunbeams and dancing on the waters' diamonds, they would join the other fairies of rank and begin training for d a lifetime of service.

Today near her own everlasting, Grandmother Fairy was teaching the magic of each color. A group of fifteen or so, who had been to the Rose Pool, gathered to hear her lesson.

"And now, dear ones, imagine the blue of the delphinium. Yes, see it! Let it vibrate through you." Her gentle manner comforted them as they struggled to learn this new skill.

Lemon spoke up: "What is a delphinium?"

"Oh, my, Lemon, you do not know your flowers yet. We will learn them together. There are no silly questions." She touched Lemon on her cheek. "I know, let us ALL transport to the Fairy Coach's garden … Close your eyes, imagine his lovely pansies…. Good … Close your wing pods and away." Now she closed her triple wings; first the rose pair, then the pair the color of dawn, and finally the purple ones. And she slipped through time.

The pleasant pop of wing pods opening! All fairies appeared in a half nothing right in the middle of the sky blue pansy patch. The fairies drew closer as she caressed a blue pansy's face.

"Now focus on this sweet flower's blue. Breathe in her lovely hue ... let it vibrate all through you to your very wing tips." She observed her students soaking up blue. "What do you feel?"

Vermilion replied first: "I feel calm."

"Exactly perfect! This is the gift that blue brings us." She lifted off the ground a foot or so and hovered over the blue pansy bed. "When the Creator brought all the colors into this world, there were only a few shades of blues. As time went by, he developed so many varieties and shades. Now there are more blues than any other color. Can you imagine why?"

"Grandmother Fairy," said Garnet, "Perhaps because humans need more calm?"

"Excellent answer, Garnet, but I do not really know. We would have to ask the Creator." She chuckled so her wings jiggled with laughter. "Let us journey over to the delphiniums."

With no effort she glided across the garden to the Fairy Coach's porch. The fuchsia bushes – salmon and dark pink – hugged the porch railing. While the clematis – still blooming in pink and white – covered the roof, the delphinium spikes burst forth in royal and midnight blue and nearly reach the rooftop. The Coach had clearly mastered the art of using the Creator's energy to grow things.

As the fairies assembled, Grandmother Fairy continued her instruction. "Fairies, let us focus on this midnight blue. Breathe it in ... Good ..." She wanted all the fairies to learn to drink in each color and its unique vibration. "And what do you feel?"

Lime raised his hand, "I feel the midnight sky is … it is a calming feeling, but it has a … I cannot quite say it."

Another voice said, "Yes, yes. Midnight blue has the calming and grandeur and yes even the peace of the heavens." He paused for dramatic effect as he often did. "Good morning, Leuria, good morning fairies. Lu, why did you not tell me you were coming?"

"Oh, Ruppy I mean Coach, Fairy Coach, we just came on the spur of the moment." She held his hand tightly for just an instant and let go. She did not want to embarrass him in front of the other fairies. But if one looked very fast, his wings flashed pink and so did hers.

Putting on a wide-brimmed straw hat, The Fairy Coach continued, "Yes, yes! Some shades have special qualities that are difficult to express in words. The Creator has given us many new colors perhaps because in this time there are so many challenges. As you know from your training, the Creator never gives a challenge without a solution. And sometimes, even though we already have many healing gifts, we have to create a new one right on the spot."

Garnet asked, "Fairy Coach, what if we create the wrong one?"

"You are sounding very much like a human, doubting yourself," said the Fairy Coach as he sniffed the honeysuckle vines.

"Garnet just came from visiting Tam's students," added Grandmother, "and they are filled with doubts."

"Yes, yes. Lu, Garnet needs a little cleaning." Grandmother eased next to Garnet and extended her first set of wings full length enfolding Garnet's. Everyone watched enthralled since they had only heard about clearing wing smoke. After Garnet closed his eyes, the darkened wing color returned to its natural clear, deep red.

94

He hugged Grandmother then asked, "With respect, sir, I just do not want to violate Fairy Cannon: First, Do No Harm."

"Yes, yes, of course. But remember when you ask the Creator for help for another, your answers are always perfect. Even if they appear to be WRONG, they have a reason, a reason you may not see at first. Trust that he is working through you. We are after all the invisible hands of the Creator, are we not?" He cupped his hand to his ear waiting for a response.

"Yes sir! Yes sir!" said the fairies in chorus.

While the Fairy Coach sat down on the top step Grandmother Fairy, Leuria, was resting against the porch railing. The fairies gathered in closer.

"Ruppy!" The Fairy Coach scowled at her. "I mean Fairy Coach." He flashed her that rare grin. "Perhaps you would review the main colors and their uses."

"Of course," He took off his straw hat and let it rest on his knees. "As we all know, most fairies are pink, red, orange, yellow, green, blue, purple or white. Pinks bring love and self-love."

Grandmother Fairy eased out to the garden and extended her third set of wings, the color of dawn pair. Then she let them spread out like a huge bellows and a pink mist filled the air. The young fairies gasped with delight. Grandmother blew gently and the mist burst into a rain of transparent cherry blossoms.

"Ohhhh, ahhh," fairies exclaimed. She waved her wings like a great cape and it vanished.

The Coach continued, "Reds bring in energy, vitality and passion." Grandmother visualized red, fanned her wings and a red mist replaced the pink one. Then she directed her great wings, iridescent red poppies exploded into the sky. Just a quickly they were gone.

"Oranges bring nurturing," the Coach said. Those giant wings flapped gracefully, and an orange mist filled the air.

"Yellows, clarity and intellect." With another stroke Grandmother imagined yellow, and all saw a yellow mist.

"Greens give us healing and teaching," the Coach continued. Leuria closed her eyes, saw green inwardly, and that color appeared. With her wings she directed it to the young fairies, and they were enveloped in green. Some rushed out as if they were playing in a spring shower.

"Blues, peace, calm and serenity," and Grandmother light up the garden with blue. "Purples, divine wisdom," and purple flooded the garden. The fairies were dancing and flying in the mist like children play in the sprinklers.

"Why does Grandmother need her wings to send color?" asked Green.

"Good question. She uses her mind to visualize the color, but her wings send the color where she wants it," the Coach explained. "Watch…"

Grandmother Fairy Mother created a sphere of blue light fanned her left wing; it twirled in front of her and moved slowly to the rooftop. She pointed her right wings, and the blue erupted into blue lupines. Then, she imagined a spiral of red, with her right wing she pointed, it rotated around the fuchsias, and illuminated red poppies scattered across the roof.   With her mind she saw yellow, and it appeared as an egg shape that started spinning. As she directed her wings toward the young students, the yellow light settled over them and the light showered daisies all over the fairies. They squealed with delight. The light broke into a million pieces and exploded with yellow, red and blue sparkles streaked with gold and silver. As the light show diminished, she let her wings sweep across the garden erasing the display. She contracted them to normal size as easily as breathing and flying. After she moved smoothly back to her position on the porch next to the Coach, the fairies burst into chatter.

"I've never seen anything…Why would you… Do you think some day…?" They were all talking at once. When the coach put up his hand, they stopped abruptly.

Grandmother Fairy began, "I've had extensive training over the centuries, but perhaps one day one of you will develop these abilities. And perhaps one of you will develop other abilities."

"Now, we will continue." He nodded to Leuria. "We are seeing a few fairies being born white for prayer and purity; a few silvers for truth; and a few golds for confidence. We cannot know what the Creator has in mind, but I image these new shades are adding their vibrations to the palette of possibilities.

"As you practice sending color you will be able to create a green shower for healing; blue to calm; pink to bring love and so on.

Vermilion asked, "Fairy Coach, then why do we all have different shades?

"Because the Great Fairy and the Creator have chosen a human charge for you and your exact color will bring out the best in your charge. It will assist your human on his or her path. Listen to your heart and it will reveal to you the unique gift of your color. In time you will come to understand the color of your destiny." He held up his hand and pulled what looked like a green bowler out of thin air. "Let's play a game."

The Coach whispered something to Lime and Lemon. They immediately began to pace back and forth. Lemon pretended to look at her watch, while Lime said, "We'll never get there on time."

Grandmother Fairy motioned for the two blue fairies, Azure and Royal, to come forward. "It is easier for the blues to send blue because that is their nature. Just as yellow is easiest for Lemon. So, Azure and Royal will start the practice… Think blue and feel blue and send blue to us." The two squeezed their eyes shut … a moment or two passed … then, a small puff of blue appeared and was gone.

"You had it. What happened?" asked Grandmother.

"They were trying too hard," replied the Fairy Coach. "It is in your wing fiber to send color. You are only waking up the gift that is already inside you. Again, breathe. Let the color float from you. Be the blue."

Then, in fairy flash a blue cloud surrounded all as a calm settled over Lime and Lemon. Their stress vanished and they smiled peacefully.

"Good! Open your eyes and see what you have created! Yes! Yes! Excellent!"

Next the Coach whispered instructions to Royal Blue. Royal moved like a slug to the cottage steps and slumped over. "I'm exhausted!"

Garnett closed his eyes and a stream of red flowed into the blue fairy. Royal sat up and hummed almost immediately.

"You see, red gives vitality," declared the Coach.

"Grandmother, how will we know when to send color?"

"Oh, you will know! Some of you will see a color in your mind; some will see a color around your charge. Others will sense what your charge needs. Remember fairies, you cannot make a mistake. There are no side effects as with human medicines. When you send the right color, you will see improvement in your charge immediately."

Garnet wanted to know: "Grandmother, I have seen you send several colors at once: green, silver and gold."

"Yes, that is possible, but it takes much more focus of the mind. You may be able to do that also if you practice and it is in your destiny."

The Fairy Coach began, "Practice so every shade is as easy as the color of your true nature."

CHAPTER 21: GROWING FAIRIES

Just then all heard the invisible hum of wings – something like hummingbird wings but much faster and higher. Near the fuchsias two wing pods formed, and in barely nothing, two fairies opened them and appeared. Grandmother Fairy's wings flapped and fluttered; the younger fairies gasped.

"Good day to all, " said Rose and Pink as one voice. The two linked arms and glided toward the porch. All the fairies were staring now, their wings, that always vibrated, were unusually still.

Rose sensed their astonishment: "What is it?"

"She is still Rose and I am Pink."

Putting her hands their heads, grandmother stated, "You lovelies are a full head taller now." Rose and Pink just beamed. Still they were not as big as Grandmother Fairy, one of the largest in the Kingdom.

The Fairy Coach added, "Usually we fairies grow gradually. We can see by your rapid growth that Tam's students must have been almost empty. They must have needed buckets of love."

Rose added, "Pink orchestrated the whole class, sir. He was our leader."

Pink reflected, "I could feel these humans pulling the love out of me. I have never felt anything like it." He glanced at Rose and she nodded. "And we both felt such love pouring into us, then going out just as fast."

Just then, the tinkling of delicate bells! And a pink golden sunset glow that was the Great Fairy's enveloped them. As the bells grew nearer everyone looked around.

"Where is she? Do you see her? Not yet."

Her bells sounded like they were coming from the garden, so all the fairies turned around. And, there hovering over the mombretia was the Great Fairy; she was fingering their deep orange blossoms. Her wings without number fanned out behind her.

Using one graceful motion of her arm she turned slowly all the way around; her subjects understood and all flew over and made a proper circle around her. A heavenly glow surrounded her and all felt her smile deep inside. In the warm silence she greeted each fairy.

After many minutes passed, she said: "Great day, fairies! Great day!"

With a joy known only among the fairies, they all said, "Good day, Great Fairy, good day!" That joy was all to them, nothing more was needed.

She began, "This day is a special occasion. Again we have witnessed the Creator's hand," smiling as each one. She motioned to Rose and Pink to come forward. They glided into the circle and stopped just in front of her. She placed her hands on the two fairies in turn, and then Rose moved to her left and Pink to her right.

"Dear fairies, so many humans have forgotten that they are loved … How to open their hearts again? WE know that fairies offer love but how else could fairies help? I have felt for some time that we had a special role in transforming this human condition. And today we have seen success.

"We now know that working as a team, fairies can accomplish much more. Rose and Pink are a natural team and, of course, other fairies assisted them. That added power and possibility to their work."

She put her arms around the brother and sister's shoulders. "These fairies so loved Tam and her students that they could do nothing but feel loved. This Rose and this Pink, indeed, they have grown overnight... faster than we have ever seen."

The Fairy Coach flew over and whispered into the Great Fairy's left ear. After she gave an approving nod, he said: "Perhaps this is because of the great need we ALL sense in humans.

"Fairies, we have much to learn about working in teams. Traditionally, we have worked alone, one fairy to one human charge. But never have we done our work in groups. Now, we see an entirely new possibility."

Grandmother Fairy added, "As Rupford was just reminding us, when the Creator gives a challenge, he offers a solution."

And the Great Fairy glided over to Grandmother Fairy and whispered, they both smiled and nodded. They said simultaneously:

Rose said, "There's something else, Great Fairy."

"Yes," the Great Fairy replied.

"Pink called the spirit of the human, Victoria."

"Remarkable," The Great Fairy said. "Is that so, Pink?"

"Yes, it just happened. We were pulling out her sadness, and... I did it for another too, Sylvester Matthews," Pink said with a shy smile.

The Great Fairy merely said, "Amazing! This bit of the Creator's magic is cause for celebration. When one of us has a new ability, it is available to all of us. Well done, Pink, well done. We are transforming as well as our human friends. This is an unusual day indeed!"

CHAPTER 22: ROCKY ROAD

"I smell something burning," cried Tam as she and Victoria raced up the flagstone steps to Victoria's house.

"Me too," Victoria rushed to unlock the back door. "Gabriel!....Gabriel! Where are you?... Are you alright?"

Victoria dropped her briefcase and dashed into the living room; Tam ran up the stairs two at a time. Almost before Tam finished, Victoria ran into Tam's room. Victoria rounded the corner of the L-shaped room and found Tam pressed against the windowpane staring down into the backyard. Victoria pulled and tugged at the old window, but it was stuck. Finally, she hit it hard with the heel of her hand and it opened. A thick black smoke poured inside so they couldn't even see the trees let alone the ground. Victoria and Tam both started to cough.

Waving the smoke away, Victoria shouted into the yard, "Gab, are you alright? Gabriel, what's burning?"

Gabriel's voice answered, "Hi, Mom! I'm fine!"

"What's on fire?" Victoria yelled trying to stay calm.

"We're barbecuing! Come on down and join us."

Tam and Victoria ran back down stairs, through the hall and out into the yard. There, standing over the old family barbecue was Sylvester Matthew's.

Wiping his brow with his red bandanna, Mr. Matthew's began, "The smoke will die down after this grease burns off. Then I can start the coals."

Quickly Victoria glanced around at her dried out bushes, the brown grass, the brittle flowers. "You could have burned down the whole block!" Turning to Gab, she said, "What are YOU doing?"

"Eating rocky road ice cream. Want some, Mom?" Gab smiled broadly. Sitting at the wooden picnic table, he licked a tablespoon and dug out another bite from the gallon carton.

Victoria, flushed with anger, grabbed the garden hose, and blurted out, "You should be..."

But Tam grabbed her arm and whispered into her left ear, "May be there is a blessing in this.... Breathe! Let us take a moment to find out what is really happening here, before we rush to punish someone."

Mr. Matthew's walked over and shook Victoria's hand, "I know I haven't been to your home before now, but I thought the boy could use some fun!"

Victoria, still startled that her yard was filled with smoke, turned the faucet on.

"Mom, Mr. Matthew's came to the door and asked me what I'd like to do. I said barbecue." Gabriel was all smiles and took the few steps from the picnic table to the faucet to give his mother a hug.

Mr. Matthew's joined in, "I said I'd like to eat rocky road ice cream. So we have combined forces." He turned his back on the smoldering grill. "You haven't used this in so long. We'll be ready to cook in a short while." He continued scraping the grill, then he added, "Victoria, I brought you some roses."

On the table was a giant bouquet of Sylvester Matthew's' beauties -- white, rose, lemon, garnet, vermilion and pink ones -- sitting in a coffee can. Victoria had been admiring his roses for years.

"Mr. Matthew's, you've never given a single rose away in your life." Angry tears welled up in her eyes. All her frustration was about to pour out.

Mr. Matthew's had not ever said a kind word to Victoria or Gabriel. Many times Victoria had tried to strike up a conversation, but Matthew's had just waved her off. Many nights she'd cried herself to sleep. He was just one more reason she felt alone.

Again Tam whispered: "Mr. Matthew's is here now, and he DID bring you his prize roses. Show your gratitude and he will learn you appreciate it. He will want to do it again. Show your anger, and he will go back to being angry."

Victoria blinked and said, "Thank you very much!" She turned off the hose and sat down next to Gabriel. Sylvester Matthews was humming a little tune as he worked.

CHAPTER 23: CAUGHT IN BETWEEN

Rose and Pink closed their eyes and pictured Tam. Then Rose vibrated her wings, formed her pod; Pink did the same. They slipped through time, green, blue and pink phosphorescence streaming by.

"Rose, I smell smoke. I cannot see anything. Where are we?" Pink's wing pod began to spin out of control.

"Rose, I cannot open my pod. Rose? Rose!" But Rose did not answer. Her pod was veering off course as well.

Back in the Fairy Coach's garden, Grandmother Fairy grabbed the porch railing and sat down hard on the flowers. She did not even notice she was accidentally squashing two clematis blossoms.

"What is it, Leuria? What? You look pale," The Coach, Rupford reached for Leuria's hand and squeezed it gently.

"I feel a sinking feeling, fear. I think I am feeling fearful." Fairies were never afraid. In fact they had a difficult time understanding this very human emotion. Leuria had only felt it a few times in her long life.

"Breathe! Breathe!" Rupford instructed her gently. "Go inside and see where it is coming from. Clearly you are picking up someone who needs our help."

Leuria, like any fairy of rank, had learned to keep herself clear of negative emotions. However, when the Great Fairy looked into Leuria's wing fiber eons ago, she recognized Leuria's far-seeing gifts. Later, when Leuria had received her second set of wings, the Great Fairy began her careful instruction. She trained Leuria to calm herself so she could trust what she was seeing and hearing inwardly. Now, no other triple winged fairy had such inner seeing or hearing. Leuria had both, and the Creator used them in times of great need.

Rupford walked Lu to the porch stool, "Sit down, dear, and look inside."

Leuria began to cough, "I smell smoke like human fireplace!" Again fear began to take her over. She grabbed Ruppy's hand. "I feel Rose; she's terrified. And where's Pink? I do not see Pink!" Her eyes flew open alarmed. "I must go to them! I must GO now! They are in trouble! They are in trouble!"

The Fairy Coach Rupford took both of Leuria's hands, "You are sure! I do not doubt you, but look again so we have all the information your vision can give us." He pulled up the other porch stool and sat next to her their knees touching. He rested his hands rested on Leuria's knees as she closed her eyes and cupped her hands over them to help her focus. Of course she wanted to know everything she could, but another part of her was afraid to look.

"Ruppy, oh, … I just see smoke. I feel awful. If I felt this for very long I would be sick," Leuria's hands moved to her stomach that was beginning to ache.

Rup put his hand on her shoulder. "Yes, Leuria, we try to coach humans to let go of their fears and trust the Creator will care for them. But they usually do not listen. If they do not refill with the Creator's love, they DO get sick… Now, focus, Lu, where are they?"

Again Leuria's eyes flew open. "I do NOT know. I do NOT see them."

The Fairy Coach Rupford stood up, walked down his porch steps and into the sun. He let his wings vibrate full speed, lift him slightly off the ground and then land. "Lu, I will go immediately."

"But where will you go? You do not know where to vision? Where are they?"

"I will go to Tam. Rose and Pink will be with her. They will have gone to her. ... Yes, they will be there, I know they will." But he too felt something strange.

Leuria floated down passed the snowball hydrangeas although she wasn't looking at them. Her mind was far away, her great wings drooped.

"Please, let me know they arrived safely. Please!" She reached out to him, and they held each other. Their wings stopped for a long moment and enfolded the two fairies. Then Leuria took two steps back. As the Fairy Coach Rupford pictured Tam, his wing pod began to form.

"I will let you know! I will!" She watched the silvery pod form, close around him and dissolve into the air. The hum of his wings lingered in her ears. He was gone!

Grandmother Fairy, Leuria, who comforted so many, now had to comfort herself. She lifted off and glided to the roof covered with pink and white clematis. There she rested mid-air letting the sun nourish her wings and her very being.

Taking long slow deep breaths she began, "Creator, your pink and white flowers remind me that the impossible is possible. The impossible is possible." She said it out loud twice to remind herself it was true. "I trust that Pink and Rose are in your care... but let them be alright, let them be alright."

CHAPTER 24: REVIVING THE GARDEN

The Fairy Coach did not wish to startle Tam so rather than envisioning her face he pictured a tree and felt seated on one of its branches. When thoughts of Rose and Pink invaded his mind, he refocused on Tam and the tree. It could be damaging to think of several things at once while travelling. Purple and green phosphorescence sped by him; his mind took him where he wanted to go. The Fairy Coach Rupford felt bark beneath his feet. He opened his wing pod slowly so he would not knock himself off the branch. He felt reassured.

This gray and tan bark feels familiar, yes, sycamore. What is that awful smell? Smoke! What in the world?

He could barely see the ground below but couldn't quite make out the scene. And he could not see Tam. Down in the yard Gabriel held onto the hose tightly while Victoria turned it on full force.

"Now wash everything off, and the water will pull out the smoke." Victoria instructed her son. After hosing the flowers and bushes, Gab shot the hose straight in the air dousing the sycamore thoroughly.

"Yikes! That is very cold!" the Fairy Coach cried out and Tam strained to hear where the familiar voice was coming from. The Coach was so startled that he lost his balance and landed with the thud right in the ice cream carton. Stunned the Coach instinctively tried to vibrate his wings splattering ice cream all over.

Equally stunned Tam blurted out, "Are you alright? Are you alright?" She wanted to laugh at the undignified landing but she did not dare. Instead she grabbed a plastic glass of water and poured it over him giving him a quick rinse. At the same time she gazed around the yard, no one had noticed. They were all busy dancing in the water.

"What are you doing? What are you doing?" yelled an upset fairy.

"Just giving you a little rinse with clean water," Tam replied recognizing the Coach under the milky cream she exclaimed, "I am so sorry, I expected to see Rose or Pink." She couldn't help smiling broadly.

"Yes! Yes!" And he produced a white hanky to mop his wet face and clean out the water from his ears. Then he vibrated his wings ultra-fast to dry them. After several moments the Coach regained his composure and dried his wings enough so he lifted slightly off the table. "I am quite fine! Quite fine indeed." Looking around he asked, "But where are Rose and Pink? Where are they?" He could not disguise his concern.

"Fairy Coach, I do not know. They left for the Fairy Kingdom some time ago. I thought you were one of them transporting back." Tam was still keeping her eye on the humans. They had not noticed her side conversation.

The Coach continued, "Rose and Pink transported, but where?"

"Sir, they have not arrived." Tam sank down on the bench her head down. "What has happened?"

"I do not know, I do not know! That is why I am here!"

Tam looked up and Victoria, Gabriel and Sylvester Matthews were standing around her.

"Who were you talking to?" Gabriel asked.

Tam stared into their kind faces. Should she? What to tell them? How to tell them? After a long few moments, Tam answered, "I have two friends and I do not know where they are."

"How do you know?" Mr. Matthews voiced his concern.

"I have a feeling…" Tam pulled her knees up to her chest and rocked.

Gabriel added, "A gut feeling you mean." Tam looked puzzled. "Like you know something in your stomach."

Tam's shoulders sagged, "There is nothing I can do."

Sylvester Matthews brightened up, "Oh, yes there is." He grabbed Tam's hand and Victoria's. He asked, "What are your friends' names?"

The Fairy Coach whispered something in Tam's ear, as Tam eyed the coffee can full of roses. One was just the color of Pink and one of Rose. Tam loved them so much a lump came up in her throat as she said, "I call them Rose and Pink."

"Let us send our love and positive thoughts for Rose and Pink then," and Mr. Matthews closed his eyes.

The Coach put his hands on Tam's shoulders; she was listening to the transformed Mr. Matthews.

"Creator, we ask you to look after Tam's friends, Rose and Pink. They are lost, but we know you are with them, so they are not truly lost. Bring them home safely. We know this is so. And, Victoria, please lift her up. She needs your strength."

Victoria had tears running down her cheeks; The Fairy Coach was beaming.

Gabriel said, "You used to be so mean!" Victoria grabbed his hand.

Inwardly Tam moaned, *I want to go home. I have caused this. Two I love more than anything are lost on my account. I have violated Fairy Fundamentals.*

Tears ran down her desolate face. The Fairy Coach glided around to face her. Tam expected a lecture, but he took her face in his hands and instead said,

"Dear Tam, this is part of the Creator's plan. When your heart hurts it is difficult to see the good deeds you have done. Because of you Mr. Matthews shared his roses and his joy again, because of you those children believe in themselves, because of you this woman has hope, because of you these neighbors discovered they need each other, because of you Rose and Pink grew in ways we did not think possible."

He looked deeply into her eyes and smiled his biggest Rupford grin. He wanted to scoop her up and take her home, to pour her chamomile tea, to show her his latest crop of firecracker lilies. He wanted to tell her what was in his heart, that he was as proud of her as a fairy, but even more, of her as a human.

After Mr. Matthews surveyed the garden, he added onto his prayer:

"Creator, please let new life flow into this garden." He winked at Tam, "and may we too bloom and grow as we do your work." Then he sat down next to her and whispered into her ear, "I have an idea. Tomorrow, why don't we…" He dabbed Tam's eyes carefully with his red bandanna while he tried to take her mind off her friends.

Meanwhile, the Fairy Coach shot up from the picnic table, past the sycamore, over and through the dead daisies. He was whizzing around the flower beds, diving in and out of the bushes, swooping around of the trees, winding invisible streamers of colors. Ribbons of golds, greens, blues, yellows, silvers trailed after him as he flew faster and faster than he'd ever flown. He stopped mid-air and lighted on his sycamore branch to survey his work.

"Red, they need red; they all need a shot of energy."

And he took off again red streamers pouring out of both hands weaving the Creator's light around each person. Truth be told, he had never done such streaming before. The divine inspiration just came to him out of the fullness of his heart.

He hovered again and exclaimed, "Huzah! Huzah!"

Then he threw scoops of gold and silver sparkles over all. Indeed his heart was so full of love; he took off again and spun yards of colors in all directions.

Tam let her heart speak. "I feel such joy all of a sudden like the Great F ..." her eyes got wide and round. She stopped mid sentence. "As if the Creator were here filling us and this garden."

Suddenly, the Fairy Coach was at her side whispering in her left ear, "Let them participate in this creation. Then, these humans will know they can create with us."

Tam felt renewed, "Yes, yes, now close your eyes and see inwardly his light pouring into you as if a great jar of warm, comforting oil were being poured into the top of your head and loving your whole being."

Good, now the garden, do not forget the garden, the Coach added.

She saw all this makeshift family smiling. "Now see this garden filled with flowers, and butterflies, and birds, yes birds... Good! Good!"

The tickle on Victoria's nose made her open her eyes. She batted something away. She craned her neck around and shouted, "Look! Look everyone!"

"Oh my, my!" was all Mr. Matthews could say.

"They are blue and yellow and brown and orange. Oh, I have missed them! There are dozens, not one or two, dozens," Gabriel began chasing them. "Mom, butterflies. The butterflies are back. Those are monarchs; the yellow and blue ones are swallow-tails." He raced around the yard chasing them.

CHAPTER 25: PREPARATION

Later that night, as Mr. Matthews drove his red pickup out of the driveway; he shoved the gears into drive and let his tires squeal just a little. He grinned and looked around sheepishly.

"I haven't done that since I was a kid," he said.

He floored it all the way down to the stop sign. Any one of his neighbors looking out the window would have thought a teenager was hot rodding. They would have been shocked to see Old Man Matthews with his blue baseball cap on backwards.

At the store he practically skipped up and down the aisles. He stopped at the potting soil and pulled out his garden sketch from his bib overall pocket and propped up on the shopping cart so he could refer to it.

The fairy voice managed to say: "Roses bushes! Rose bushes," into Matthews' left ear. The charge stopped at the stack of bare roots raised bushes but moved on.

Sporting a blue baseball cap, the Fairy Coach tried again: "Roses, your garden needs roses; your garden needs roses. You are so stubborn!!"

Finally Mr. Matthews shouted, "Alright roses. And I'm not stubborn!"

The Fairy Coach replied, "Good, roses! This one's a tough cookie, but he listened."

For no apparent reason Mr. Matthews took off his ball cap and used it to swat something off his shoulder sending the Fairy Coach in a brief nosedive. But the unflappable Coach recovered and flew back

116

to his charge's left shoulder. An out of breath Fairy had a moment to catch his while Matthews examined the bare root fruit trees.

"Fruit trees will give lovely blossoms; fruit trees will give lovely blossoms," said the Coach. And Matthews heaped an apricot, a peach and a fig tree on his growing mound of supplies.

Then Matthews was off again almost running. After his first shopping cart overflowed with 50-pound bags of soil, shovels, clippers, and boxes of giant trash bags, he quickly filled another pulling one and pushing the other happily. As he buzzed down the aisles, he was mentally scanning his potting shed and garage for what he had on hand and what he needed.

"Something in bloom is very healing, something is very healing," the invisible helper whispered.

And Matthews stopped at the bulb display. He counted out dozens of daffodils, narcissus, gladioli, anemones, and ranunculus into small paper bags. He fingered some tiny bulbs no bigger than his thumbnail. He read the label: "Firecracker lilies!" And he counted out a dozen into a small bag. The Fairy Coach tipped his ball cap with approval.

"We'll have red, yellows, whites, purples, blues," said Matthews visioning the garden in full bloom.

He'd occasionally flick his left ear and send the Fairy Coach skittering and then flying to catch up to his charge. When Matthews finally maneuvered into the checkout line, he didn't even look at the total bill. Usually he was adding up the total on his calculator to make sure he stayed within his budget and to double check person at the cash register. He delighted in finding errors almost as much as he did getting a bargain. But tonight he'd forgotten all that. He just slapped down his credit card.

"Ring it up, son," Mr. Matthews beamed.

The red headed clerk in a crisp white shirt and red apron said, "Mr. Matthews? Is that you, sir?"

"Yes, Donald, didn't I have you in senior biology? What you doing working here?"

"I'm working here all night to put myself through college. What are you doing here at midnight?

"We're going to replant Victoria Moreno's garden in the morning. Great fun! Great fun! It's going to be a healing garden."

"WOW!" The boy was more shocked at Matthews himself than with the late hour. "Sir, with all respect sir, you …you look so different …you even sound different."

Mr. Matthews face was lit up like he was in love and he'd been on vacation. He quickly signed a credit card slip and pulled something else out of his wallet.

"I was pretty hard on you, wasn't I, Donald. I am sorry."

That was the first time he'd apologized in longer than he could remember. He took his former student's hand and pressed something into Donald's palm.

"Here, maybe this will help a little."

Donald opened his hand and gasped. "Mr. Matthews, I think you made a mistake; this is $50."

"No mistake young man; you're worth every penny!"

Mr. Matthews was already heading for the door. Donald ran to catch up with him. "Thank you, sir; I don't know what to say. At least let me help you load your truck."

The unlikely pair hoisted the bags and tools and new plants of every variety into the truck bed. By the time Mr. Matthews drove his red pick-up home, it was almost 2 AM. But this man who is usually in bed by 8:30 PM was not tired. His mind was racing with ideas for the new garden. He finally fell asleep about 4 AM.

CHAPTER 26: THE SEARCH

While his new charge slept, the Fairy Coach sat cross-legged on the hood of Sylvester Matthews red pickup deep in thought. His work with Mr. Matthews had not lifted his own spirits as fairy work usually did; he was still gravely concerned about losing Rose and Pink.

He knew better than to try to fly between realms when his mind was not clear, but he had to try. He folded his first wings, then the second pair; he held Pink and Rose in his mind; his wing pod formed. Blue, purple and pink streaming filled his vision; he was racing between, but worry consumed him. He barreled end over end getting quite dizzy.

Rose Pink, Creator, Rose and Pink, he thought. His course straightened out.

Maybe my beloved fairies are stuck somewhere, suffocating, even dead. No, not dead! His pod went spiraling without control.

Great Creator, help me! Help me! He yelled. Rose and Pink, Rose and Pink.

Plop! He opened his wing pod and fluttered full speed to orient himself. He landed right on a huge pink rose in Sylvester Matthews' garden.

"Ouch!" He said pulling out a thorn. "Not these roses, Rose and Pink, Rose and Pink."

Determined, he repeated this process twice more, but he always landed back on the pink roses.

A bit dizzy and very frustrated, he stretched out on the warm metal of Matthews' red pickup and gazed at the stars.

"Creator, I don't know what to do. You who have created all life, indeed, all of us..."

His voice trailed off. The always-vocal Fairy Coach did not know what to say. He folded his hands behind his head; it was the closest to despair he'd ever felt. He searched the midnight canopy hoping just one of the stars might give him an answer.

Go home! Go home! He heard softly between his own thoughts.

The Fairy Coach began pacing back and forth on the pickup roof.

"Yes, yes," he burst out. Standing still with his hands on his hips, "I will go immediately."

Don't look for them with fear; let your love guide you, he heard inwardly.

He closed his eyes, filled his heart with love for Rose and Pink, and vibrated his wings rapidly. He visualized his own garden, formed his wing pod, and raced to his destination. The familiar green and purple phosphorescence streamed past him as he sped through time. Mid-stream, images of Rose and Pink invaded his mind, and his wing pod began to spin end over end out of control. Sensing the danger, The Coach opened his eyes.

The garden, my garden, he thought and his path straightened out. Then Rose and Pink popped into his head again and his pod zigzagged off course.

Oh blessed creator, my garden; my garden, he yelled. His pod was on the right path once again.

"Plop! SSK!" A little disoriented he opened his wings and found himself on a white hydrangea. He quickly turned up his wing speed and flew to the path. He saw warm lights in his own cottage window. He was home, but no Rose or Pink. With an empty heart he floated to his front door.

CHAPTER 27: THE MISSING

Leuria wrapped her wings around her Ruppy with the fullness of her heart. Without words they let their wings vibrate together, flushed deep pink, then enfolded each other. After several minutes, Ruppy moved over to his favorite chair and put his head in his hands.

"Oh, Lu," he moaned.

"Is it Tam?"

"No, no," he said. She pulled up the chair across from him. "Rose and Pink; I cannot find them. I have flown between worlds, and nothing."   Leuria put her hands on top of his and held them tightly. After a time Coach barked, "Say something!"

Leuria looked away and said, "I have no words!"

"Lu, can you go inside and look for them?"

Leuria said, "I don't think so; I am too stirred up; I cannot focus." He did not try to talk her into it.

He merely said, "I understand."

"We will look again in the morning." Leuria couldn't even bring herself to smile. Their wings drooped and were even a little cloudy.

CHAPTER 28: CALLING THE SPIRIT

The next day Grandmother Fairy and the Coach awoke before dawn and met for morning tea as was their custom.

After chamomile tea, the Coach said, "Let us greet the day."

They flew to their favorite part of the garden, the rope trees. They sat on their limb, the one they had climbed together as young fairies, to watch today's magic unfold. First the palest golds began to fill the sky followed by soft lavenders flushed with pinks. They quickly turned to bold purples, electric fuchsias, dazzling yellows, brilliant blues. The low-hanging clouds were back lit with a blazing rainbow. As the morning's first rays struck the pond, the sun exploded across the water.

"Another day the Creator has made just for us," the Coach Rupford said as he linked his arm in Leurias'.

"Ruppy, when I woke up this morning I had an idea…What if we could call the spirit of Rose and Pink?"

"What do you mean?"

"Well, Rose told us that Pink spontaneously called the spirit of two humans… that means we should all be able to do it. Yes?"

The Coach lifted himself off the branch and flew out a few yards disturbing a flock of sipping birds that burst into flight and wheeled skyward.

He hovered in front of her, "Yes, but how would that help them?"

"I'm not sure, but I have a feeling .. Suppose somehow they lost their spirits between worlds. And we cannot find them because we can't find their spirits." The Coach fluttered his wings rapidly and then paced back and forth through the air as he did when he was thinking. Leuria continued, "Well, if we could call them back, then..."

The Coach filled in her thoughts, "Then we could find them wherever they are." He cruised over beside her, "But we have never done this before."

"I know."

"And we'd be doing magic for beings long distance. We'd have to invent it."

"I know." She linked her arm in his. "But we have a great need, and we have great love, and we have the Creator's help." Hope filled her and she smiled. She instinctively fanned her color of dawn wings and cleared the grayish wing smoke from both of them. Their luminescent wings sparkled again like they had been newly washed in a spring shower.

"Great Fairy, we need to talk to the Great Fairy," Ruppy said. Almost immediately, they began to hear her tingling bells mixed with the breeze. Out over the pond a tiny pinpoint of light began to come closer; it steadily grew as her music settled over them. When her bubble of light suspended right in the front of them, she seemed to emerge from it.

"Good morning, dear ones," she said.

"Good morning, Great Fairy," the Coach and Leuria responded simultaneously.

"Let us go to the Grand Meadow Center," and the Great Fairy was already flying toward it. The Coach and Leuria eased off their perch and floated after her.

Wisdom filled decisions were made at the Meadow's Power Center, and today they needed all its help. The Great Fairy turned slowly letting her wings without number gracefully drape over the pink peonies and yellow scotch broom. Those wings caste a light of their own so a sphere of radiance extended around her. Enveloped by her light, the three high ranking fairies stood facing each other.

The Great Fairy began, "I have looked for Rose and Pink inwardly also, and I see nothing. That is a puzzle to me, but I do sense they are alive."

"Oh thank goodness," blurted out Leuria.

"Now, what do you propose?

The Coach, said, "Leuria thinks we should call the spirits of Rose and Pink."

"I see," She closed her eyes to consider this. All of her wings suddenly fanned out and stiffened like a giant peacock's tail. After several moments, her eyes flew open.

"What is it?" Leuria asked. She'd only seen the Great Fairy's wings stand up when she had to look deeply with her every wing fiber. Indeed this was such an occasion. Leuria had to watch herself to keep her mind calm and clear.

The Great Fairy finally spoke, "Yes, it can be done. We should all do this calling the spirit together." They closed their eyes and took many clearing breaths and began to focus. "Creator, we ask for the highest good and greatest service of Rose and Pink."

Instinctively, they each moved back making the space between them bigger. After several minutes, a gold haze hung in the air accompanied by a reed flute. The flute's lonely melody seemed to call up two white trellises that climbed slowly into the air, and then joined together forming an archway. The three moved back even more sensing the creation needed more room. Another flute joined the first playing gently as if coaxing two vines to grow slowly and steadily up, winding, until they met and intertwined. The fairies stared breathlessly. They could now see a single bud on each vine.

Slowly, slowly the buds began to open as the flutes encouraged them to grow. Even the Fairy Coach was transfixed.

As soon as their colors were recognizable, Grandmother Fairy burst out, "They're pink!"

"Hush, hush," the Fairy Coach glared at her.

Clearly, one flower was becoming pale pink and the other, deepest rose. At their fullest bloom, the Great Fairy let her wings without number stand up.

She said, "Go, go home to the Fairy Rose and the Fairy Pink."

As if following her command, the flowers floated from their stems, and hung overhead for several moments side by side. The flute duet stopped abruptly. The flowers started spinning faster and faster and vanished into thin air.

"Magnificent!" the Fairy Coach was the first one to find words. An invisible force pulled the vines and trellis back into the ground.

The Great Fairy simply said, "The Creator's work is always inspiring."

"But where are they? Where are they?" Leuria said.

"We must trust that they are in the Creator's hands," the Great Fairy let her wings wrap around Leuria. The Coach joined them. All their wings fluttered and flushed pink.

The Coach said, "We will find them; we will find them."

CHAPTER 29: THE DAWN

The exuberance and festivities in Victoria's garden kept Tam's mind racing. She was tossing and turning long after she'd gone to bed, so it was close to dawn when she finally drifted off to sleep. When she first came to Victoria's, she'd had many sleepless nights. Tam would climb out onto the roof and sleep under the stars; now she just slept with all the windows wide open. She even wore an oversized plaid nightshirt that Victoria let her borrow. At least then she was descent by human standards even though it hung to the floor.

She felt a buzzing around her head and swatted at it. Whatever it was tickled her nose again.

"Go, away," she said with her eyes still closed.

A familiar voice said, "I am not a house fly. Good day to you, Tam. Come see the day the Creator has made."

Flitting around Tam's bedroom, the fairy couldn't help inspecting the jackets neatly hung on hooks, the two pairs of tennis shoes, the school books stacked on the desk. At the dresser he found a comb, hairbrush, even makeup.

How very organized, how human she has become, he thought.

She sat bolt upright. "Fairy Coach, greetings. I am sorry."

"How very human of you to bat me away like a common bug. Many humans do not appreciate the gift of fairy assistance even when it flies in their faces," he scolded her.

"I AM sorry; I AM sorry," Tam said again standing up to shake the sleepiness from her body. She once dreaded his scolding, now she welcomed it. She dared not ask about Rose and Pink.

He took her arm and guided her as she walked to the window; he flew to the roof and waited.

"Come greet the day; it is only a few steps," the Coach encouraged.

Tam swung one leg over the sill, stepped onto the shingles, then climbed to the roof's peak. She sat down next to the Coach facing east. He tenderly linked his arm in hers.

The sun was just brushing the sky with her morning colors. The soft pinks sprinkled with blues grew brighter by the minute. The buttermilk sky shimmered gold, the pinks turned to crimson. A heavenly artist painted the sky especially brilliant today. As the day began to break, the palette began to fade into pastel pinks and grays, then the dawn. By the time the sun peaked over the eucalyptus trees these vibrant hues would become the sky's daily blue.

"A red sky in the morning, it will rain later today. Another sunrise the Creator painted just for us. Most humans miss this daily splendor," the Coach said.

"Thank you, I have been so busy with the job of being human, I had forgotten to celebrate the glory in the everyday." After several minutes, Tam continued, "When can I go home? When can I go home?" Her whole body longed suddenly to see Grandmother Fairy; her wing attachments ached to fly through her everlastings.

"You must replant her garden, you must replant her garden," the Coach said firmly.

Tam balanced herself on the roof and said, "Yes, I know. I need go to school early and get Thomas' gardening tools."

Tam picked up the hem of her flannel nightshirt and stepped back into her bedroom.

"Do not forget to ask if you can borrow them," the coach called after her. Truth be told, he was proud of her.

CHAPTER 30: DRESSING

Tam turned on the cold water full blast; the ice cold shower always invigorated her. She toweled dry, smiled at her human self in the mirror, and fingered her hair in place.

"These humans have so much to do just to start the day. Back home I'd be dancing on the waters' diamonds already," she said.

She threw on Victoria's striped overalls, tied her tennis shoes in double knotted bows, and bounded down the stairs. Learning the habit from Victoria, she caught a quick glimpse of herself in the hall mirror to check her appearance.

"Humans have so much attention on looking just right, and I am fast becoming one of them," Tam said softly. She licked her finger and pressed down a stubborn strand of hair.

She paused at Victoria's bedroom door, knocked and entered. Her human friend was still buried underneath her down comforter snoring like a tea kettle.

"Victoria, Victoria, I must go to school early. Goodbye."

A sleepy voice answered, "See you later."

"I know you like flowers. We are going to replant your garden today, is that alright?"

"Sure, sure," a muffled voice said from deep under the covers. "I have to take Gabriel to the doctor."

Tam closed the bedroom door carefully so it would not slam. She learned that from being human as well. So many details about how to be thoughtful, what was the correct way to dress, how to behave properly -- far more human rules than Fairy Fundamentals.

"Fairy Fundamentals seem easy compared to all the human ones," Tam said as she locked the front door behind her and put the key in its hidden spot under the first flower pot. She'd left the door unlocked several times, but she had learned this habit as well.

The Fairy Coach, hands folded across his chest, strutting up and down on the rain gutter. "Well, I'll be! I never would have thought it possible."

'Fairy Coach?" Tam looked up to see him turning up his wing sped, lifting himself of the ground, and pacing midair. "Coach, I could use your help today, please."

"Yes, yes, I do not want to miss this. I will be there, I will be there."

"Thank you, thank you," and Tam was striding down the walk to school.

Flying as far as the lamppost, he mused, "She even said please and thank you. She makes a better human than I did."

CHAPTER 31: THE TOOLS

The sun was already burning off the morning chill, when Tam ran most of the half a mile to school. She gazed at the San Gabriel's clearly still visible before the afternoon smog's haze concealed them. She knew Thomas started work long before anyone else did. As she approached the 800 quad, she saw his orange custodian's cart.

"Thomas, Thomas," she called.

She saw his wild garden gate standing open and walked inside. Stopping to catch her breath, she said, "Good morning."

Thomas was kneeling near the coral-bells pulling weeds.

"Good morning, Tamara; what are you doing here so early?"

"I need to borrow your tools," she panted.

"Sure, Thomas said. "How long do you need them?"

Neither of them saw the two silvery wing pods caught in the redwoods' branches just overhead. The pods were hopelessly tangled in the branches, somehow stuck together.

"Just for today. I'm taking my class to Victoria's and we're replanting. Mr. Matthews is going to help, he's being awfully nice to Victoria and Gabriel and me." Fingering the tissue paper-thin petals on some white flowers, Tam asked, "What do you call these?"

"They are from the poppy family. My kids call them fried egg flowers with those yoke-colored centers," Thomas answered.

"They are prettier than fried eggs," Tam said.

Thomas leaned up against the fence. He peeled off his gloves and slapped them together to get the extra dirt off. That didn't work so he slapped them against the young tree sending its slender trunk and branches rocking. The pods began to sway.

Thomas continued, "WOW! Old man Matthews? Nice? That would be a miracle. Do you have school permission to go off campus?"

"I have the Creator's permission," Tam said boldly.

Thomas stomped his boots to get the dirt off, then bracing himself against the fence, he tapped his soles against the trunk. This sent the pods rocking back and forth widely.

"I don't want to track dirt all over the school and into the classrooms I just vacuumed." He paused. "I heard Mrs. B. is coming back soon, that means you'll be leaving us. You've done wonders with her class of ruffians."

Tam tried to gather up the shovel, spade, and hoes. "Thanks, Thomas, thanks."

"I'll drive you to your room," Thomas said. "Matthews used to yell at his kids so loud you could hear him clear across the quad. I'd like to see this nice Sylvester Matthews."

They stepped onto the asphalt, he locked the gate, and they drove off.

CHAPTER 32: THE REPLANTING

By 8:30 am Tam was walking her class to Victoria's garden each student carrying his hoe or her shovel or one that Thomas had loaned Tam. Miss Tamara Rupford and Evie had on overalls, but most wore jeans and old T-shirts. Today Miss Rupford allowed ball caps and hats, but no gum. As her crew marched up the driveway, she stood and handed out tissues to each student who still was chewing.

"Spit it out, please," Miss Rupford ordered. They all put their gum in the Kleenex and put it in the trash barrel; not one gave her a hard time or talked back.

Mr. Matthews greeted them: "Good morning, good morning to you all," he yelled in his old cranky voice.

"What is he doing here?" said Carmen under her breath.

"Be kind," coached Miss Rupford hands on her hips.

"Yes, Miss R," and in one swift motion Carmen rubber banded her abundant brown hair into a ponytail.

Tam said, "He is here to help us do a good job." Talking to her whole class now, she continued, "Some of you have probably had Mrs. Moreno; this is her house. Her son Gabriel has been dreadfully sick."

"Miss Rupford, I didn't know he was sick; I just thought he was skinny and white all the time," said Howie.

The Fairy Coach said so only Tam could here, "You are Miss Rupford? You took my name!" He beamed that rare Rupford smile hovering over the dead daisy bushes.

Mitch said, "Old Man Matthews?" Mitch pulled out a cigarette lighter and fingered it. He slipped it back in his pocket unseen. Mr. Matthews picked right up on Mitch's comment.

He bellowed, "Yes, I am a little old, but I am better at biology than you." Then he broke into a huge grin, "I'll bet you I can weed and plant faster than you. I have a pair of gloves; water bottle; and a red, green, blue or yellow sticker for each of you. Sign in here. No one goes home until you sign out and give back my gloves." He held up his clipboard. "Now, Miss Victoria Moreno and her son have had some hard times; they have no family. So we're here. Let's get this job done and have some fun while we're at it."

Mr. Matthews had taken dozens of field trips with students, so he had his time line and team assignments taped to the garage wall along with his garden plans. He had his list of tasks, potting soil, trash bags, even band aides. First, they had to pull out all the dead plants and weeds; then, they'd have to prepare the soil; then planting and watering. If they worked very fast, they might be done by the time Victoria came home from school.

He looked skyward, "By the looks of those buttermilk clouds, it will rain later."

"How do you know?" said Howie.

"The front that's bringing the rain is starting to collide with the dry one causing that buttermilk sky. The clouds are even darker and thicker than they were at dawn. Next time you see that you'll know to take your umbrella," Matthews said kindly putting his hand on Howie's shoulder. "Howie, you're on the Red Team, stand over there please with Evie. Everyone stand with your team, by the section that is your color." No one moved. Matthews blew his old PE whistle and the kids jumped and they moved. "That's better." He blew the whistle twice again softly. "Now, we're on a tight time line, we have one hour to pull out all the dead bushes, weeds and trees. Everything dead goes in your color-coded trash barrel. When it's full empty it into the dumpster in the street. I have pizza, ice cram and movie passes for the team that wins. Ready, go!" He clicked his stopwatch.

"You've done this before," Tam said admiringly.

"I've done trash clean ups with kids at rivers and beaches for years, but never anything to help a family." Mr. Matthews walked over to help Howie pull out a stubborn bush. "Mitch, take your shovel and loosen up the dirt." Mitch did as he was told. Mr. Matthews looked up to find Laurel starting to throw leaves at Carmen.

"Anyone goofing off sits out and your team loses," Mr. Matthews shouted so loud Carmen plugged her ears, but she stopped throwing leaves and started pulling weeds. Already Blue Team had a barrel full to take to the dumpster. "The good news is the dried up plants should come out easily." He put his arm around Tam, "Your job is to encourage each team and make sure they are on task."

Tam looked around and everyone, yes everyone, was either pulling up dead flowers, or tying up bags of trash, or loosening up dirt. She and Matthews smiled at each other, "Tam, I can't thank you enough. I'm having a great time."

"Oh no, thank you, Sylvester Matthews."

Just then Tam heard a familiar hum behind her; she gazed around for the Fairy Coach. He was flitting from team to team adding blue energy to some and pink to others. But Tam turned toward the hum and saw a wing pod forming behind the picnic table.

It has to be Rose and Pink, she thought.

And she casually took the few steps across the yard. The huge pod began to open, first one pair of wings, then another and another.

"Grandmother," Tam burst out.

"Yes, Tam, I am here," said Grandmother Fairy. She hugged her great-granddaughter quickly. Tam glanced over her shoulder to make sure no one had noticed, but all her students were too busy.

Mr. Matthews blew his whistle, "OK, first water break. Everyone stop and take at least two gulps of water. We must keep hydrated." Matthews blew another two soft whistles, "OK, back to work." All the students obeyed, put down their bottles and went back to work.

"Tam, I see Rose and Pink's pods," said Grandmother.

"Oh, thank goodness, thank goodness. Where?"

Grandmother closed her eyes and looked inward, "I am not sure, but they are hanging in everlastings somewhere in the human realm. It's a small garden with flowers that look like fried eggs." She opened her eyes, "Do you know such a place?"

"Yes, yes, I do. Its Thomas' wild garden."

"We must go immediately, immediately," Grandmother declared.

"Yes, but my students," Tam said. By now the Fairy Coach was at Tams' side.

"I will stay here with Mr. Matthews and keep these kids organized. They are ALL doing very well, very well. Go now, and find our Rose and Pink," the Fairy Coach said.

Tam caught Mr. Matthews by the sleeve. "I must talk to you now, please, privately." They stepped away from the student workers.

"Yes, Miss Rupford," Matthews said.

"I must go to school now; it's important, it's an emergency. I'll be back as soon as I can. Can you manage for a little while without me?"

"Yes, of course, how hard can gardening be? I've done this for years. Look around, the kids are working and they even look like they are enjoying themselves a little." Mr. Matthews said putting his hands in his bib overalls and pulling out his red bandana handkerchief. "Is everything alright?" He blew his noise.

CHAPTER 33: THE DASH

Grandmother, I cannot transport," Tam yelled as she dashed out of the garden gate and broke into a full run. Grandmother flew along behind her wings trailing like gossamer kites. Tam raced faster than she'd ever run in her short life as a human: her lungs were burning by the time she turned into the campus driveway.

As she approached her own 800 quad, she heard over the loud speaker, "Miss Tamara Rupford to the office immediately, Miss Tamara Rupford to the office. Sorry for the interruption."

"No, No! Grandmother, we do not have time for that," Tam puffed.

"You must obey the human rules, Tam, you must," said Grandmother, and Tam knew she was right.

"But Rose and Pink," Tam stopped to catch her breath.

"I will go to the wild garden you described. I can find it now," Grandmother was trying to sound kindly but she knew finding them was urgent. Rose and Pink had been gone longer than any fairy in the history of the Fairy Kingdom.

Tam pulled open the main office door, and said, "I am here. What is it that you want?"

Dr. Krause leaped up from her desk, spilling her pencil can and her coffee mug all over, and yelled, "Miss Rupford, and where have you been? And furthermore, where is your class? Mrs. Wagner, can you clean this up for me?" The ever-ready school secretary was already pulling out the papers towels from her desk drawer.

"Oh that. I took them to Victoria's garden and we are replanting. It's a wonderful lesson in contributing to others, don't you think?" Tam was still breathing heavily.

"Miss Rupford, you cannot take students off campus without permission from parents and from me. Don't you know that?" Dr. Krause was shocked. She'd been very pleased that Miss Rupford truly been teaching this class something, but this.

"But Dr. Krause, you should see them. Mitch and Carmen and Laurel and Howie and the others, they are all working very hard," Tam pleaded but she realized she was in trouble.

Dr. Krause roared, "You violated about 17 school district policies. And where are your children now?"

"Oh, I left them with Mr. Matthews. He's a teacher too," and Tam ran out the door and headed for the wild garden.

Dr. Krause seemed to settle down a bit, "Yes, I know. We're taught together for 25 years." But Tam was already out of ear shot. "Well, Mrs. Wagner, make sure that this is Miss Rupford's last day even if we have to get another substitute."

"But, Dr. Krause, Miss Rupford is the only sub who has been able to get class doing actual work," Mrs. Wagner observed.

"I don't care. Get rid of her," said the angry principal.

CHAPTER 34: THE PODS

Tam found Thomas' orange cart parked near the cafeteria. "Thomas, Thomas, I need you," Tam yelled.

Wearing a denim skirt and school T-shirt, a teacher Tam did not recognized stepped out into the quad and said, "Quiet, please, we are taking a test today."

"Sorry, sorry, but where is Thomas?"
Carrying his tool box, Thomas stepped out from that classroom, "I am right here."

"Oh, Thomas, I need you to unlock the wild garden for me."

"Now? Right now?" Thomas put his arm around his friend. "We're right in the middle of class. Can't it wait until after school?"

"No, no, this is an emergency. I have two friends who are dying and …." Tam's voice trailed off and she could hardly hold back the tears.

"OK, OK, jump in," Thomas said. He put is tool box in the back end, and they drove off.

Thomas struggled to find the right key to the pad lock.

"Please, hurry, hurry!" Tam was close to panic.

After several tries, Thomas found the right key and unlocked the pad lock. Tam pushed the gate open wide and searched around for her Grandmother. Tam heard the flutter of wings and looked up.

"Oh, no," Tam gasped and put her hand over her mouth. There, caught in the young redwoods were two wings pods. Grandmother had tried to land right on the branches, but her weight sent them swaying so she took up her vigil midair. Now she was holding them tenderly and vibrating her wings so she could maintain her almost still position.

"Thomas, we need a ladder," Tam was staring upward; Thomas obeyed.

"Tam, he must not know I am here, he must not," Grandmother said.

"But he believes in fairies and elves, Grandmother," Tam pleaded.

"That may be true, but he will have enough to deal with in a few moments if all goes well," Grandmother replied.

Thomas returned saying, "OK, Miss Rupford, now what? I still don't know what's going on?"

"Put it here, right under the tree," Tam ordered. And she climbed up to ladder to its top step and reached up to the pods. But she was too short. "I cannot reach them, I cannot."

"Thomas, you must, you must," Tam instructed.

"I must what? I don't get this," Thomas answered. He was confused.

Grandmother, he needs to see them, he needs to see them. We need his help, Tam shouted in her mind.

Grandmother flew over behind Thomas and put her hands over his eyes.

"Thomas, what you are about to see is going to blow your mind as my students say; but we need you, the fairies need you. Do you remember you said you believed in us?" Thomas rubbed his eyes. "Well, look up there in the redwood."

Thomas glanced up and looked at Tam again. "Is this a joke?" Grandmother held her hands over Thomas's eyes again.

143

"Look again, Thomas, look with your heart," Tam urged.

And Thomas gazed up into the trees. "I see something. What on earth? I see something silvery," he said.

"Yes, yes. Please, Thomas, I cannot reach them, you must climb up and untangle them." Still not sure what this was all about, Thomas followed her directions. "Be gentle."

Thomas worked to free the pods. "Something sticky has glued the branches to them, but I think I can get this thing loose. Get me my pruning shears from my tool box," he said.

Tam was off like a shot and back with the shears in a fairy flash.
She climbed the ladder and handed them to Thomas. He gingerly clipped away some branches carefully. When the pods were finally free, he cradled them carefully and stepped down.

"What do we have here? Miss Rupford, what are these?"

Tam was guiding Thomas hands and helping to place the pods on the ground.

Tam, we need to open them quickly, Grandmother said inwardly.

Tam saw were they were sealed closed and began to try to pry them apart. Their silvery covering was smudged with smoke and smelled like fireplace.

"They seem glued shut. How can we get them out?" Tam said.

"Who? What are these? Is there something alive in them?" Grandmother Fairy moved over to the pods, enclosed them inside her wings, and then jerked her wings apart.

Tam, see if that lets you open them now, Grandmother said.
Tam tried again to free her hopelessly stuck friends.

144

Thomas said, "Are these things something from outer space?"

"They are not things, they are my friends. Thomas, they are fairies." But Thomas was pulling gently on one end of a pod and it began to give. With his stronger hands he tore open a tiny two-inch gap.

"Be careful, be very careful," Tam said.

"The ends seems a little easier," and Thomas stepped over the pods to try the other end. He pulled firmly and another gap opened up about 3 inches.

Grandmother eased in over the pods, enclosed them with her wings, and jerked them open again. One gave way and snapped apart like a pea pod.

"Try it again," Tam said. "They are almost free." Tam's heart was beating triple fast. She twisted her hands and pulled at her clothes like a fairy in distress. "Quickly, they may be already...." She couldn't bring herself to say it.

Thomas grabbed the seams firmly and tried to pull them apart.

CHAPTER 35: MITCH

A few hours later, Victoria tried to pull her car into the driveway. It needed washing so badly that a student had written WASH ME on the dusty window. Victoria found that Mr. Matthews had her driveway blocked with his card table, trash barrels, bare root trees, roses and other flowers, so she had to back out.

She rolled down the window and shouted, "Mr. Matthews, Tamara told me she was planting flowers, but I had no idea you'd be here. And, where did all these kids come from?"

Mr. Matthews, who was sorting plants by section, said, "Mrs. Moreno, welcome home. We wanted to surprise you. This is Miss Rupford's class." Gabriel jumped out and Victoria pulled her car up to the curb.

"Mr. Matthews, Mr. Matthews, it's gone, they can't find it." He grabbed Sylvester Matthews around the waist and hugged him long and hard.

"Terrific!! That's great news," Matthews smiled.

Victoria walked up to the duo and said, "What are you doing?"

"I'm organizing the next phase of our replanting. Gabriel, you could take these colored dots and put them on the right plants. Here are my charts, one for each section. All these plants get red dots for the red section," Mr. Matthews said.

"I get it, and then the blue dots go on the plants for the blue team, right?" Gabriel knelled down and began his project. He was thrilled to feel good enough to help.

"Look, all these students have come to help you," Mr. Matthews said taking Victoria by the arm and guiding her into the yard.

"Hi, Mrs. Moreno," Laurel said. Mrs. Victoria Moreno pulled out a tissue and whipped a tear away. All she could do was wave to Laurel.

Matthews blew his whistle twice, and everyone stopped and took two gulps of water. "I have an announcement; or rather the Moreno's have something to tell us."

"I can't talk right now; this is too much," Victoria said. "You tell them, please."

"Everyone, Gabriel's tumor is gone!"

The Fairy Coach shouted, "Yes! Yes!"

The girls applauded; Howie gave a thumbs-up; other boys gave the touchdown sign with both arms straight up.

"Congrats, Mrs. Moreno," said Evie.

Victoria took a long swallow of water to try to holdback the tears. Finally, she found her voice and said, "The scan this morning showed nothing. They even did it twice, nothing, zip, zero. I am so thankful you are all here, thank you."

Howie, walked over to Gab, "You can be on our team." He had already moved a folding beach chair over to their section. "You can sit down when you get tired."

"Mom, can I?" Gabriel was already in position with Red Team.

"Sure, fine, but take it easy," Victoria said. 'Mr. Matthews, did you organize all this? Who bought all this? You?"

Suddenly, the Fairy Coach was flying right in Matthews' face and waving his arms frantically. He pulled on Sylvester Matthews' ear, but all the biology teacher did was brush him away. The Coach persisted and pulled on Matthews' other ear; harder this time.

"Ouch!" Mr. Matthews rubbed his ear. "Something just bit me."

"Look over at Mitch, look over at Mitch," the Coach yelled.

"I smell smoke," Victoria said scanning the dry tender that littered her yard.

Carmen pointed toward the house, "Mr. Matthews, over there!"

Mitch was squatting down under the camellias. He was lighting a tiny flame under one bush; two others were already burning; flames were already climbing up the garage wall.

"He'll set the whole house on fire. Call 911, call 911," screamed Victoria.

Mitch started to run for the gate, but two students caught him by the knees and wrestled him to the ground. Gabriel grabbed the hose.

"Turn on the water," yelled Gabriel. Howie obeyed.

Evie leaped up and ran to help Gabriel; they both grabbed the hose and began to spray the rapidly spreading fire.

CHAPTER 36: ROSE AND PINK

Trying not to cry, Tam was cradling Pink and Rose in her lap rocking them gently just as Tanny had held her when she had been ill. That seemed like a life time ago.

Thomas said, "They are still breathing. Let's move them over into the shade."

"No, no! They are both so cold. They need sunlight to recharge and nourish their wings," Tam said. She couldn't hold back the tears that were running down her cheeks. Even though the two fairies were gray; their faces, sunken; their wings wrinkled; they were alive.

Grandmother Fairy said, *Calm down, calm down; you are no good to them upset.*

Tam said, "They moved a little, but they are such a sick color. What should we do?"

Thomas sat down crossed-legged next to Tam, rubbed his hands together, and closed his eyes. He stretched out his big hands over the weak fairies.

"Creator, I ask that you send your light through me into these gentle beings," Thomas said.

"My friend Finne from the Elf Kingdom used to do that for me," Tam said.

Thomas said firmly, "You must be quiet so I can stay centered."

Immediately, Grandmother was right behind Thomas pouring her light into him. The very weak fairies began to pull it from Thomas. Just then they heard three long school bells.

Thomas opened his eyes, "That's my bell, I am needed somewhere on campus. But we must take another minute or two." He took a long deep breathe and refocused. Pink and Rose stirred and even rustled their wings a bit.

"Its working, Thomas," Tam spirits lifted.

"Do not move, it will break my connection. Your friends are taking a great deal of healing energy right now," Thomas said still eyes closed. After a long time Pink and Rose opened their eyes.

"Where are we? What happened?" Rose said.

"You are in a school garden with me, Tam, and my friend, Thomas."

Rose sat up and looked over at Pink. She took his hand and pulled him to a sitting position. As Thomas clasped his hands together, he said, "Thank you, Creator."

"Who is this?" Rose said.

"Thomas, he helped me save you. You were caught in these everlastings and he got you down."

 Still invisible, Grandmother Fairy moved around them so she could put her hands on the recovering fairies' heads and continued healing.

"Pink, I remember now," Rose was still holding his hand. "We could not see anything but smoke. The smell was horrible. We tried to visualize you, Tam, but we could not. Our pods kept going off course."

Pink said, "And all I could think of was our everlastings in the home forest."

Tam said, "So you must have transported to these everlastings by mistake." Rose and Pink's wings began to flutter and they spontaneously lifted off the ground a foot or so. "The color is coming back to your faces."

They both flew slowly around the garden as if for the first time, then returned to hovering just in front of Thomas.

"Thomas, we thank you," said Pink.

He responded, "I have asked to see my spirit friends since I was a boy. I am very grateful." Three more long bells blasted across the school grounds.

"I must go," Thomas stood up. Before he drove off, he turned and but his hand on his heart and smiled. "I will never forget this day."

Pink said, "Grandmother Fairy, I did not see you."

"I remained hidden because of our new friend, Thomas; he had enough to deal with just seeing you," Grandmother replied. She let her huge wings hug both fairies. "Now, Tam, we must all get back to Victoria's garden. Rose and Pink and I will fly along with you so they can get their wings back in shape. You are both looking better by the minute."

"Thank goodness you are safe and alive," Tam said. "I am so glad to see you." Rose and Pink were at her side.

CHAPTER 37: FIRE

As Tam sprinted across the park and down the street, she saw heavy smoke and heard sirens.

"What in the Great Fairy's name?" Tam said.

As Tam walked around the corner, she found red fire engines and a black and white police car with its light flashing pulled up in front her home. She raced the half a block remaining the fairies flying close behind her. A fireman in his helmet and yellow coat was reeling out hose from the fire engine to the backyard. All the students were gathered on the sidewalk coughing and rubbing their eyes. Some were hugging each other; others were talking among themselves. The air was thick with smoke.

"What is going on? Is everyone alright?" Tam shouted.

Mr. Matthews, who was comforting Victoria on the sidewalk, said, "The firemen are getting it under control right now. Luckily, Evie called 911 before it burned the entire house. Everyone seems to be fine, just a little shaken up."

Making her way through the smoke-filled backyard, Tam stepped over their hoses and found firemen dousing the last of the flames. Gabriel and Evie were manning their hose. Three firemen were just turning off their hoses; one fire woman was on the roof hosing down the shingles. The garage wall was badly scorched so that the once-white wall was completely blackened. The bushes were charred sticks; smoke was still rising from them.

Sylvester Matthews put his hand on her shoulder and said, "Miss Rupford, Mitch set a fire."

"Where is he?" Miss Rupford asked.

Then she recognized her student; he was face down in the dirt near the alley wall. Howie was holding down his feet and Carmen was sitting on his backside. Although the policemen had him in handcuffs, he was still struggling.

"Officer, I am the teacher here. Did this young man set the fire?"

Miss Rupford asked.

"I saw him, Miss Rupford," said Carmen.

"Then we have a witness," said the officer. "Kids, let's turn him over so I can question him." The students struggled to flip Mitch over, but still held him down. Mitch's eyes were wild like a scared animal; he was thrashing his head from side to side. But the more he thrashed the tighter the students held him.

The officer pulled out his notebook. While he interviewed the student witness and Mitch, the Fairy Coach flew over to Mitch and began to pull out sticky gray slime from Mitch's chest. Pink was at his side.

"Good to have you back, Pink," said the Coach. Pink nodded.

Pink was taking the slime and lifting it into a pale mist above their heads. The moment the slime touched the mist it turned clear.

After several minutes, Pink closed his eyes saying, "Creator, this young human needs his spirit and if this be his time,..." Pink held up his right hand. Nothing. Pink repeated the phrase. A ball of pale purple light formed in his hand, but it was very faint. Grandmother Fairy instinctively moved over and put her healing hands over the ball.

"Fill this with your light," said Grandmother. And the light grew stronger.

Now Pink took the light tenderly in both hands and said, "Go home to Mitch, go home to where you belong." And the light jumped into Mitch's chest. Strangely, Mitch's body relaxed; he stopped struggling; his eyes became clear.

Putting his notebook in his uniform pocket, the officer said, "That does it. Young man, you are under arrest for setting fire to Victoria Moreno's house." The office read him his rights and started to lead him away.

"Just a minute, officer. Mitch, you apologize to Mrs. Moreno, right now," said Mr. Matthews sternly.

An unusually polite Mitch obeyed, "I am sorry, Mrs. Moreno, very sorry."

Matthews, more fatherly than angry, continued, "You will re-paint her whole house, I will see to it you do."

"Yes sir, I will," said a very subdued Mitch. "I promise I will."

"What will happen to him?" asked Evie. By now, all the other students circled around them.

"He'll go to jail where he should be," said Mrs. Moreno. "He almost set my room on fire last year."

Matthews added, "Maybe, we all need a second chance." He winked at Tam. And the officer lead Mitch away, put him in the patrol car and drove off.

The fire chief walked over to the group and said, "The fire is out; the structure is sound; everything is safe and secure."

"Thank you. I think we should all have some lunch. Captain, please ask your crew to join us. Miss Rupford, your students must be famished," said Victoria Moreno.

"I'll order pizza," said Matthews as he flipped out his cell phone and started dialing.

Just then Dr. Krause stormed into the yard only to find she had to pick her way through the shovels, gallons cans, trowels and hoses.

"I got a call from the police," Dr. Krause said surveying the scene and the youngsters. "Everyone's OK? Good." When she locked her eyes on Tamara Rupford, she clinched her jaw muscles. "Miss Rupford, this is too much," Dr. Krause seethed. "You are fired!"

"No," yelled Evie. "She's the best. I read a whole book in her class."

"You can't fire her; we were learning stuff. I am passing all my classes now," said Howie.

Carmen said, "I liked digging in the dirt." Evie was crying quietly.

Mr. Matthews said, "Relax, Dr. Krause, these kids have had the time of their lives, and they have been working hard."

Dr. Krause glared at this new Sylvester Matthews, and said, "Have you been in collusion with Miss Rupford?"

"Absolutely, students off campus is partly my fault. Why don't you look and see what's really going on here?"

Dr. Krause couldn't yell at him, not in front of all these people. She just stood dumb-struck like the blood vessels on her neck were going to pop.

Tam glanced at the Fairy Coach who was sitting on a sycamore branch with Pink and Rose.

Can I go home now? she asked inwardly. She felt a couple of raindrops on her face.

Tamara Rupford said, "Thank you all. I have learned so much from all of you." She looked up at the coach again.

"My assignment is over here; I need to go home now."

A little calmer Dr. Krause announced, "Mrs. Brockway will be back starting Monday."

Tam said to her students, "I know you will not forget what we learned together, it will in your hearts forever." She gazed around at all their sooty, but loving, faces. Tam could not find the words to say what was in her heart.

Gabriel ran over to her and said, "This is your home."

"Gabriel, it has been, but I need to see my own family," Tam put her arms around the young man's neck.

Matthews blew his whistle twice and announced, "Kids, we still have planting to do, and we are behind schedule. Let's work until the food arrives. Blue Team over there; Red Team here. Get busy."

Quickly students grabbed their shovels and began digging holes for fruit trees. Some consulted Matthews' chart; others pushed bulbs into the soft dirt; some placed yellow marigolds and red and white petunias around the curved brick border. While Howie dug holes, Evie placed the yellow and orange lilies and Gabriel pulled them gently from their gallon cans. Sylvester Matthews placed the new camellias and Carmen dug holes for them. Even though the garden was taking shape, it would be another season or two before it was in full bloom.

Mr. Matthews and Mrs. Moreno were delighted to see these young people smiling and active. But Tam had a sad task. She tapped him on the shoulder, "I will miss you, Sylvester Matthews, and you too, Victoria. This is the hardiest part of the assignment, but I will take a part of you with me wherever I go."

"Pizza, the pizza is here," yelled one student.

After Mr. Matthews paid the bill, teachers, students and firemen gathered around the picnic table.

"Please sit down, all of you," Matthews said kindly.

Mrs. Moreno said, "This is the first time we've had so many guests in a very long time; we are so thankful for your work."

Then the hungry students and adults tore open the cardboard boxes and feasted on pizza and coke. Even Dr. Krause was chatting with everyone.

CHAPTER 38: FLYING

When no one was noticing, Tam slipped out, bounded upstairs and walked to her room for the last time. Her assignment finished, she did not want to linger for long drawn-out goodbyes. Leaving was hard enough. She climbed out of her window and onto the roof. Grandmother Fairy, Rose and Pink as well as the Fairy Coach were waiting.

"Fairy Coach, I am ready." Grandmother and the Coach enveloped her with their wings for one long moment.

The Coach held up his hand and a wand of white light appeared. "Creator, the Fairy Tam has indeed earned back the wings that you have been keeping for her." A silvery, limp blob of what looked like potato skins appeared in his hand.

Grandmother put her healing hands other them and said, "Creator, fill these wings with your life energy."

She paused and gazed lovingly at her great-granddaughter. The wings sprang to life and jumped from the Coach's hand. For a moment they hung mid-air in front of their rightful owner.

The Coach said, "Turn around, Fairy Tam."

Tam tore off her tennis shoes and human clothes and turned her back to her fairy family. The Coach brushed Tam's wing attachment twice.

"Go home to our Fairy Tam," announced the Coach. The wings danced the few inches to Tam's back and found their place right between Tam's shoulder blades. They buzzed and fluttered; Tam sat down hard.

"I remember another time you sat down like that," the Coach beamed his famous grin, held up his hand, and the wand disappeared. Perhaps the Creator, himself, took it from his fairy servant.

"I am a bit dizzy," Tam said.

"Just flutter them a little," Grandmother suggested. "You will get used to them quickly. It is your fairy nature to fly."

Rose and Pink at each elbow, Tam stood up and flapped her wings. The more she fluttered, the more her body shrank to its fairy size. After several tries, she lifted off the roof slightly. She flapped rapidly this time and raised herself several feet. Then she buzzed them super-fast.

"Can I fly now?" Tam asked.

"Of course," said the Coach and Grandmother beaming.

Three jubilant fairies took off like rockets. They flew loop-the-loops; they did intertwining spirals; they did barrel rolls. Their squeals of delight echoed through the trees. Tam shot straight up as far as she could and then nosedived almost crashing into the senior fairies. She pulled up just in time.

Exhilarated, Tam said, "That was wonderful. I had forgotten the seer joy of flying." And she took off again Rose and Pink just behind her.

"Now let us go home," said Grandmother Fairy.

Tam said, "Wait, please. I have one more thing I must do."

She took off and headed to her students, Rose and Pink followed. In a quarter nothing, she landed on Evie's left shoulder.

The Fairy Tam whispered, "Everything you need is inside you, everything you need is inside you. You are loved beyond measure, you are loved beyond measure."

She glanced at Rose who was at Howie's left shoulder whispering a fairy message. Pink was at Carmen's doing the same. The three made it around to everyone.   Then she flew to Gabriel's left shoulder.

"I will always be beside you, I will always be beside you," Tam said with great love.

After gulping down two cokes and three slices of pizza, Gabriel searched for the bare root roses. He and Howie and Evie arranged them – red, yellow, white, pink, peach and lavender -- in their section. Evie sat down on the ground and was writing something.

"Mr. Matthews, Mrs. Moreno, we want to make a rose garden for Miss Rupford. What do you think?" Gabriel announced.

Victoria Moreno and Sylvester Matthews said simultaneously, "Great idea!"

Evie took a hammer and pounded in her stake; Howie taped up the sign. It read: TAMARA RUPFORD'S ROSES.

CHAPTER 39: HOME AGAIN

Deep in the Fairy Kingdom forest, Tam slept soundly on her home port everlasting. She dreamed of basking on a rock letting the sunlight warm her fairy body and nourish her wings. Her robin friend, green breasted and double the size of the ones found in the human realm, circled around her chirping widely. Tam opened her eyes to see morning light just beginning.

"Good morning, Robin, I missed you too," she said taking a deep breath of fresh forest air. She drank in the smells of home that were like no others.

Still getting reacquainted with her fairy body, she fluttered her wings, stretched them, and turned them up to full speed.

"Honk! Honk!" She looked skyward and saw a pair of mallards flapping their way toward the pond. She took off and flew tandem with them thrilled to re-join the skies.

"Great day, my friends," Tam said.

She veered off from her feathered friends, and she lighted on the highest everlasting she could find and faced the east to greet dawn. Half perching, half fluttering, she surveyed the forest canopy from the Creator's view.

The new morning brought the soft grays, the edges of the clouds turned palest pink and blue. As the sun crept to the horizon, the pinks and blues glowed from within.

Tam said out loud, "Creator, I never thought I would say this, but thank you for the gift of being human. I have seen their despair and anger; I even felt some myself; but I never felt alone. My heart is full of love for these humans."

The dawn painted the skies with deep fuchsias, mauves and purples outlined in gold. Just as the sun broke over the horizon, Tam raced to the pond to find a spot at the water's edge. She wanted to see that moment the first light splashed across the water. In a burst of joy, she raced up its reflection as only fairies do. After, she found Grandmother Fairy and the Fairy Coach seated in their rope tree.

"Good morning, Grandmother. Good morning, Fairy Coach."

"Good morning, Tam," said Grandmother. "The Great Fairy awaits us at the Rose Pool."

"I thought we would all be at the Grand Meadow," Tam inquired.

The Coach said, "Today is only for those who have been to the Rose Pool."

From out over the pond, two fairies zoomed toward them. They pulled up along side of Tam.

Tam said, "Great day, my Rose and Pink. You are well?"

Rose said, "WE are perfect!"

With that Tam heard the pool's waterfall in her mind and pictured the Great Fairy. She formed her pod and was gone. Rose and Pink followed.

Grandmother said, "She has missed being a fairy. Our Tam is very different from the one who left us not long ago. I think she will help us deepen our understanding of those humans that are so hard to reach."

"Indeed!" said the Coach. "I still do not understand humans and I even lived as one of them."

Grandmother and the Coach pulled their wings together hummed their pods into being. They too were gone.

CHAPTER 40: CELEBRATION

At the Rose Pool the swans glided effortlessly toward the waterfall. The morning breeze caught the mist and sprayed it over everyone, but no one minded. All the fairies who no longer had their primary names had assembled just after dawn, and their wings were buzzing with excitement. Fanned out over the rocks were the fairy variations of reds, from garnet to pink; oranges, from peach to vermillion; yellows, from lemon to maize; greens, from lime to emerald; blues, baby blue to midnight; and purples, from lavender to royal. They always arranged themselves in a rainbow for such ceremonies. Just the array of light beings was splendid indeed.

The Great Fairy had planted roses for today; white, pink and yellow climbers wound themselves around trees trunks and among the rocks. Bushes covered with huge blooms in every shade imaginable – lavenders, peaches, burgundies, vermilions, even blues and shades unknown in the human world. The Great Fairy had added a new green rose this morning.

Lemon spotted her first, a point of light starting to form inside the falls. "There!" pointed Lemon. "She is coming!"

The light was growing stronger, and her essence taking form as it traveled. Her tinkling bells grew louder. Now, a ball of light hovered over all and she seemed to step out of it.

"Great day, fairies," she said letting her warmth surround them.

"Great day, great day," her subjects said.

Taking her place over the shale above the falls, she held out her arms and motioned to Tam, Rose and Pink. They flew to join her.

"Today, we have much to celebrate. Our Fairy Tam has come home to us richer for having lived as a human." She touched Tam on her head. "Fairy Tam, take this white rose and dip it into the Rose Pool."

This was most unusual because Tam had already been to the Pool and received her true destiny color, emerald, although everyone still called her Tam. Tam did as she was instructed, knelt at the water's edge and dipped her perfect white rose. It turned silver. Gasps rippled through the fairy community. Then she flew back to the Great Fairy's side and placed it in the crystal goblet that the Great Fairy was holding. The clear water turned a silvery shade. Several fairies lifted off the ground to see more clearly.

"Drink this Emerald Fairy Tam and become even more of your true destiny."

Tam drank the silvery liquid completely and handed the empty goblet back. The fairies held their wings utterly still. Nothing seemed to be happening. Tam's wings buzzed and stopped, buzzed and stopped. Nothing. More fairies lifted off the ground to get a better view. Then tiny streaks of silver began to travel down her wing veins. Tam flexed her wings and stretched.

The Great Fairy put her hand on Tam's head and announced, "Tam has become a green with silver; the silver is now in her very wing fibers. We have never seen such a color combination, but then again, we have never had a fairy like our Tam. Her destiny is as a green, the healing and teaching color, and as a truth speaker, a silver."

Even though Tam ached to test her new wings, she only lifted off a bit. She stopped herself from racing to the skies to be respectful of the ceremony.

The Great Fairy said, "Fairy Pink, come to Center."

"I am here, Great Fairy," Pink nodded.

"Show us what you have learned," the Great Fairy commanded.

Pink closed his eyes and held out his right hand. "Creator, I ask to call the spirit of the human." He paused. He needed a name. "Gabriel." A ball of pale pink light began to spin in his hand. "Go home! Go home to the boy, Gabriel." And the orb lifted off, spun rapidly and vanished.

Usually silent at ceremonies, the fairies broke out into chatter: "What does it mean? How will this help? Can we do this too? How does he do that?" The Great Fairy raised her hand, and silence fell over them again.

The Great Fairy began, "Pink asked to help his human charges, and the Creator answered. We know that when one of us masters something new, it is available to all. Although that happens rarely anymore, we have seen it today. Fairy Pink?"

Pink nodded and talked his light friends through the simple process.

Then he said, "Ask for the spirit of a human that you love. Say his or her name, just as you would if you were calling the spirit of a flower or tree."

Every fairy had a ball of light in his or her right hand. "Now," Pink said, "Tell your light spirit to go home to that person."

And all the light balls rose up, spun rapidly, and exploded like a thousand soap bubbles. The orbs had transported to their human hosts. A rush of fairies flew over to Pink and embraced him. Again the Great Fairy raised her hand and sent them back to their places.

"Once again, by allowing the light to work through us, we have been the Creator's invisible hands. Now, Fairy Pink, for demonstrating leadership and creativity in helping your human charges and for mastering a new ability,..." She held out her left hand and her wand appeared. She shook it lightly three times, and a limp set of wings appeared. As the fairies started to cheer, since many had never seen a second wing ceremony, the Great Fairy held up her wand for quiet.

"Creator, fill these wing with new life for our Fairy Pink." She tapped them and they came alive like tiny hummingbirds. "Turn with your back to me, Fairy Pink." He did has he was told.

"Wings, go to your new home." The Great Fairy tapped Pink's wing attachments and the wings magically fastened themselves right between his shoulder blades. They buzzed and stopped. Then the two pairs buzzed together for the first time.

"We have a new double-winged fairy," announced the Great Fairy.

"Hurray! Hurray for Pink!" shouted the whole assembly.

Pink's friends and relatives could not contain their joy anymore; they swarmed around to congratulate him. The Great Fairy nodded to Grandmother; Leuria eased over behind Pink, Rose and Tam. The triple-winged fairy pointed her great wings and a cloud of pink light hung over everyone; she blew gently into the cloud and it burst into a shower of cherry blossoms. Then she threw out puffs of pink like cotton candy and blew silver sparkles into them; they turned into cherry blossoms streaked with silver ribbons. For several minutes all the fairies were transfixed on the pink and silver celebration.

After a long time at the pool, Grandmother took Tam by the elbow and they floated to the rope trees overlooking the pond.

"How does it feel to be in your fairy home again?" Grandmother inquired.

Tam said, "Wonderful but strange. I came to love my human family so that I miss them. That is a human feeling, is it not?"

"Very much so," said Grandmother. For a long time, they just sat enjoying each other's company and the warmth of the sun.

Then they heard familiar music; they both looked in the direction of the Great Fairy's bells. Her ball of light emerged from the pussy willows and drifted over the pond toward them. As she eased in front of the rope tree, they could see her light extend to include them. Tam closed her eyes for several minutes to drink in that fairy feeling she had missed in the human world.

When the Great Fairy finally spoke she said, "Welcome home, dear Tam. How is it for you?"

"Great Fairy, I am so enjoying my wings and the pleasures of just being home in the Fairy Kingdom." She paused, "May I be honest, Great Fairy?"

"I expect nothing less from you, Tam," she replied.

"I do not think dancing on the waters diamonds and serving invisibly will ever be enough for me."

"I had hoped you would say that," said the Great Fairy. "After you have rested and visited with your friends and family, I wish to meet you and your Grandmother again here at the rope tree."

"Great Fairy?" Tam wanted to speak, but the leader's face faded quickly right in front of them. She vanished.

Grandmother instinctively said, "What did you want to tell her?"

Tam said, "Two things, no three things. Thank you. I have so much compassion for the humans."

"And the third thing?" Grandmother Fairy urged.

"Sometimes, I just want to shake the humans and say WAKE UP!"

They both laughed so hard that their wings shook.

Made in the USA
Middletown, DE
04 June 2022

66575168R00097